D1559117

Living in Sin

Look for these titles by Jackie Ashenden

Living in Sin

Jackie Ashenden

Samhain Publishing, Ltd.
11821 Mason Montgomery Road, 4B
Cincinnati, OH 45249
www.samhainpublishing.com

Living in Sin
Copyright © 2014 by Jackie Ashenden
Print ISBN: 978-1-61922-825-2
Digital ISBN: 978-1-61922-221-2

Editing by Christa Soule
Cover by Lyn Taylor

This book is a work of fiction. The names, characters, places, and incidents are products of the writer's imagination or have been used fictitiously and are not to be construed as real. Any resemblance to persons, living or dead, actual events, locale or organizations is entirely coincidental.

All Rights Are Reserved. No part of this book may be used or reproduced in any manner whatsoever without written permission, except in the case of brief quotations embodied in critical articles and reviews.

First Samhain Publishing, Ltd. electronic publication: November 2014
First Samhain Publishing, Ltd. print publication: May 2015

Dedication

This one's for the Ashendens.

Chapter One

"She's here again."

"Oh fuck, really?" Kahu Winter leaned back in his office chair and stared at Mike, the bouncer who'd been working the door at the Auckland Club for the last five years.

Mike, a huge Tongan guy who used to do a lot of pro-wrestling, folded his arms. "Yeah. And she says she wants to see you."

Since that's what she'd been saying for the past couple of nights, Kahu wasn't surprised. Jesus Christ. What a pain in the ass.

He had more important things to do than fuck about dealing with Rob's daughter. The guy was Kahu's business partner and would not be happy at the thought of his twenty-year-old daughter hassling for entry into one of Auckland's most exclusive private-member's clubs.

What the hell was she doing here? What the hell did she want?

"That's the third time this week." Kahu threw the pen he'd been toying with back down on his desk. "And I'm getting pretty fucking sick of it."

Mike was unimpressed. "Perhaps if you go out and see what she wants, she'll go away," he pointed out.

Not what Kahu wanted to hear. Christ, the last two nights he'd paid for a taxi to take her home and if she kept this up, it was going to start getting expensive.

Of course, he could go out there and speak to her. But he liked being manipulated even less than he liked being told what to do. And he *hated* being told what to do. Especially when the person doing the telling was a spoiled little twenty-year-old on some mysterious mission she wouldn't talk to anyone about other than him.

Jesus, it made him feel tired. And pretty fucking old.

"Goddamn. I'm going to have to speak to her, aren't I?"

Mike lifted a shoulder. "Up to you, boss."

Yeah, he was going to have to.

Cursing, Kahu shoved his chair back and got up. The work he was doing, going over the club's accounts, could wait. And he probably needed a break anyway.

In the corridor outside his office, he could hear the sounds of conversation from the Ivy Room, the club's main bar and dining area. Friday night and the place was packed with members having a post-work drink or seven.

The sound of success. Anita would have been so proud.

Yeah, but not so proud of the fact you're planning on ditching it, huh?

No, probably not. She'd left him the club thirteen years ago, when she'd first realized she was getting sick. A gift he'd promptly thrown back in her face by fucking off overseas, refusing to accept the responsibility or the reality of her illness. It had taken him five years to come to terms with it. To come back to New Zealand, to take on the club, and most importantly, to care for her. The lover who'd rescued him from the streets and given him the stars.

On the other hand, Anita was six months dead and what she didn't know wouldn't hurt her.

As he approached the club's entrance—a vaulted hallway with stairs leading to the upper floors, a parquet floor, and a chandelier dominating the space like a massive, glittering sun—people greeted him. Since he granted all memberships to the club personally, he knew everyone. Some more than others, of course, but he prided himself on the fact that he knew everyone's names at least.

He ostentatiously kissed the hand of a politician's wife, slapped the back of a well-known actor, air-kissed with a socialite and shook hands with an awestruck nobody. But then that's what the Auckland Club was like. Nobodies and somebodies, all mixing together. It appealed to his sense of irony. And, fuck, it was a nice distraction if nothing else.

Kahu pushed open the big blue door that was the club's famous entrance and stood in the doorway, looking down the stairs to the sidewalk. There were no lines of people waiting to get into the club since it was members only, but tonight a lone figure sat on the bottom step, her back to him.

It was mid-winter and cold, his breath like a dragon's, a white cloud in the night.

Not as cold as London, though.

A random memory drifted through his head, of the European "cultural" trip with Anita. Of being in London in February during a snowstorm, and she'd tried to insist on going to some kind of classical music concert at Covent Garden. He'd seduced her in their fancy Claridges hotel room instead and they'd spent the rest of the evening in bed, away from the storm and the cold…

Kahu let out another cloudy breath, trying to shake the memories away.

He'd grieved when Anita had died. But the woman in that chair in the rest home wasn't the Anita he'd known and loved. That woman had died a long time ago.

The person sitting down on the bottom step suddenly turned and his drifting thoughts scattered. A pale, pointed face and eyes an indeterminate color between green and gray looked back at him. A familiar face.

Lily.

He knew her, of course. Had known her since she was about five years old, her father Rob being a close friend of Anita's, and who'd managed the club while Kahu had been sulking overseas. Who'd become a valued business partner since.

A quiet, watchful girl who stayed out of the way and did what she was told, if he remembered right. He hadn't seen her for five years, though, and clearly things had changed. Namely that she didn't do as she was told anymore.

Lily stood and turned around. She was wearing a black duffel coat, the hood pulled up against the cold, and dark skinny jeans, a pair of Chuck Taylors covered with Union Jacks on her feet. And a very determined look on her face.

"Lily Andrews, as I live and breathe," Kahu said lazily, standing in the doorway of his club and crossing his arms. "Does your father know you've been sitting on the steps of my club for the past three nights straight?"

Her hands pushed into the pockets of her coat, brows the color of bright flames descending into a frown. "If you'd spoken to me earlier it wouldn't have been three nights."

"I have a phone. Though perhaps young people these days don't use such outdated technology."

"What I want to ask you is better done in person."

"That sounds portentous. Come on then, don't keep me in suspense.

What do you want?"

She didn't speak immediately, her mouth tightening, her eyes narrowing. As if she was steeling herself for something.

Jesus, whatever it was it had better be good. He had shit to do.

After a brief, silent moment, Lily walked up the steps, coming to stand in front of him. The light coming from the club's doorway shone directly on her face. She wore no makeup, her skin white, almost translucent and gleaming with freckles like little specks of gold. She looked sixteen if she was a day.

"Can I come in? I don't want to ask you out here."

"What, into the club? Sorry, love, but it's members only."

She shifted restlessly on her feet. "So can I be a member then?"

"Are you kidding? You think I just hand out membership to any fool that comes to my door?"

Her forehead creased into a scowl. "I'm not a fool."

"If you're not a fool, then you'll understand that there's a reason it's taken me three days to speak to you."

"I just want to ask you a question. Nothing else."

"Then send me an e-mail or a text like any normal teenager. Now, if you don't mind, I have a few things I—"

"I'm not a teenager, for Christ's sake. And what I want to talk to you about is…personal."

Kahu leaned against the doorframe, eyeing her. "If it's personal then why aren't you talking to your dad or a friend or whatever? You hardly know me."

Rob had been Anita's lawyer as well as her friend. Kahu had met him in the context of dinners, where Anita had brought Kahu along and he'd sat there silently at the table while she and Rob talked, unable to join in because he didn't know what the fuck they were talking about—the dumb, uneducated Maori kid from the streets.

Sometimes at those dinners Lily had been there, a small seven-year-old with big eyes, whom he'd ignored mainly because she was a child and he had nothing to say to a privileged white kid from Remuera, born with a silver spoon in her mouth.

Then, after he'd come back from overseas and had reconnected with Rob over the management of the Auckland Club, he'd sometimes see her as he talked business with her father. A slender teen with a sulky mouth, who appeared to lurk permanently in the hallway whenever he arrived or left, big gray-green eyes following him when she thought he wouldn't notice.

She'd grown up a bit since then, the rounded features of adolescence morphing into the more defined lines of adulthood. But that mouth of hers was still sulky and she was still small and slender. And her eyes were still wide and big as they met his.

"Yeah, I realize that. But…" She shifted again, nervous. "What I want to ask concerns you in particular."

He raised an eyebrow. "Me, huh? Well, spit it out then."

A crowd of people came up the steps behind her, laughing and talking. Kahu moved out of the way as they approached the door, greeting them all by name and holding out his arm to usher them inside.

Once they'd all gone in, he turned back to Lily, who remained standing there with her hands in the pockets of her coat, glaring at him almost accusingly.

He could not, for the life of him, work out what her problem was, but one thing was for sure: he was getting bloody sick of standing there while she continued to dance around the subject.

"Okay," he said, glancing at his watch. "You've got ten seconds. If you haven't told me what you're doing here by then, I'm going to go inside and ring your father, and ask him to come and get you."

"All right, Jesus," Lily muttered. "You don't have to be such a dick about it."

Kahu refrained from rolling his eyes. "Ten, nine, eight, seven…"

She turned her head, looking back down the steps, clearly checking to make sure there was no one around.

"…six, five, four, three—"

"I was kind of wondering if you could perhaps seduce me."

The words came out way too fast and not at all like she'd prepared, which was annoying. Even more annoying when he burst out laughing as if it was the funniest thing he'd heard all year.

Still, she'd expected this kind of reaction from him and if she'd been in his shoes, she'd probably have done the same. The daughter of a business partner, a woman he barely knew, coming up to him and asking to be seduced…yeah, funny as hell. Especially when all he saw when he looked at her, no doubt, was the kid who used to hang out in the hallway at home whenever he visited her dad.

No wonder he was laughing.

Lily stayed where she was, waiting patiently until he'd finished. He was going to say no, of course, and that too she expected.

It had taken her at least a week after her failed ballet audition to make the decision to come here. A week of much soul searching as she tried to put the bitter disappointment of not getting into the Royal New Zealand Ballet Company behind her.

Your dancing lacks passion, they'd told her. *You're trying too hard. You're holding back.*

Lily gritted her teeth against the memory. The feedback had been painfully hard to take, her dreams of a dance career dying before her eyes. Because they were right, she *had* been pushing herself. She had so many missed years to make up for and the ballet world was so horribly competitive that if she wanted any kind of dancing career, she *had* to get a place in one of the major ballet companies now.

But no, one failed audition didn't mean the end. She'd beaten the leukemia that had nearly killed her. She w*ould* achieve her dreams as well.

And Kahu Winter was the key. That's why she was here. They'd told her she lacked passion? Well, she was here to find some and hopefully from him.

"Glad you're amused," she said as his laughter eventually wound down. "I guess that means no, right?"

"I'm sorry, that wasn't at all sensitive." He made a show of wiping his eyes. "But then I don't often get girls I barely know coming up to me and demanding to be seduced." He paused. "Or at least, not these days."

Lily curled her fingers tighter inside the pockets of her coat. She was cold and sitting on the steps for the past twenty minutes had made her even colder. "Can we discuss this inside now, do you think? I'm freezing."

But Kahu didn't move. "We're not discussing this anywhere. You're not a member, you can't come in. And if you're cold, I suggest you go home."

"You heard what I said though, right?"

Kahu pushed himself away from the doorframe, his arms still crossed over his broad chest. "Yeah, sweetheart, I heard. And though the offer is lovely, if somewhat random, I'm going to have to refuse."

Yep, there it was. Refusal right on schedule.

Kahu Winter was famous for his list of lovers but she knew he'd probably baulk when it came to adding her to it. She was, after all, the daughter of his business partner and quite a bit younger than he was.

Then there was the whole virgin thing, which she was going to have to tell him about, because when it came to experience, she had none and it was going to show.

So yeah, all good reasons for him to say no. Which meant she was going to have to work hard to convince him otherwise.

You could just try someone else.

A simple answer to a not-so-simple question. Because the problem was, she didn't want to try someone else. She'd been lusting after Kahu since she'd been old enough to understand what lusting meant. And even before then, as a wide-eyed seven-year-old, she'd found him fascinating. So different to the men she was familiar with. They all wore suits and spoke carefully, as if they were tasting their words before they let them out.

But Kahu wasn't like that. Tall and muscled like a superhero from a comic book, a Maori tribal tattoo on one arm, he didn't speak carefully. He didn't speak much at all and when he did, his voice sounded like he had a throat full of sand.

He was a grown-up and hadn't taken much notice of her, but she hadn't been able to stop looking at him. He was so big and looked so strong. Like he could carry the world on his shoulders. And yet, as he'd sat at dinner with her father and her father's friend, Mrs. Howard, she had the idea that he was just as bored with the conversation as she was. That he didn't understand what they were talking about either. Once, during one of those interminable dinners, he'd looked at her, his eyes full of darkness and secrets. It was like looking into a black cave and had scared her a little. Until he'd winked, making all her fear vanish. Making her feel like they were in this together. A heady moment for a child used to being alone.

For a couple of years after that, she'd hung around him whenever he visited, hoping for another wink, another sign. But he didn't do it again and then he vanished for ages, only returning when she was fourteen. By then, things had changed for her. She wasn't seven anymore and the height and muscularity of him, that impression of incredible strength, wasn't intimidating, but fascinating. And desirable in ways she couldn't quite understand.

She understood now, though. And six years later he was still just as fascinating to her, still just as desirable.

He wore plain black pants tonight and a simple white business shirt, no tie. The top buttons were undone, revealing brown skin and the plaited cord of the greenstone necklace he was never without. He had his sleeves rolled up and those black eyes were full of darkness and secrets. But there was no wink this time like there had been back then, only a kind of world-weariness that made her chest hurt.

She didn't know why she felt this connection with him when it was clear he felt no such connection to her. But that didn't change the fact that she did.

"Okay," she said, clenching her fists in the pockets of her coat. "So what can I do to change your mind?"

Possibly asking that question was the wrong move. Possibly turning up here in jeans and sneakers and a duffle coat was also the wrong move. Maybe she should have worn something short and sexy, something that showcased her legs. Something visual that would change his mind, because weren't men supposed to be visual creatures?

Then again, what the hell did she know about men? Pretty much fuck all of nothing. Since the age of seven her life had been dance and there had been no time for anything else. Then when she'd gotten sick, her life had been hospitals, catheters, IV tubes and chemo. Definitely no time for the opposite sex there either.

Kahu's dark gaze was impenetrable. "Nothing," he said succinctly. "You can't change my mind."

Great. Well, she'd never shied away from the hard truths and she wasn't about to start. May as well know she wasn't his type straight-up now. "So I'm not attractive to you?"

His eyes narrowed. "Jesus Christ. You're totally serious about this, aren't you?"

"Of course I'm serious. You think I'd spend three days sitting on your step then randomly ask you to seduce me for fun?"

"I have no idea since I don't know you from a bar of soap."

The words slid a barb under her skin unexpectedly. He wouldn't know her, that was true, and why would he? His contact had been with her father. He had no reason to know her. Yet she felt like she knew him. Totally erroneous, of course, since they'd never sat down and had any heart-to-heart chats or anything. But she still felt it.

"I'll give you a hint then," she said, trying not to let the hurt show. "I'm not a bar of soap."

The corner of his mouth curved in a faint but very definite smile. "True. You're not." He paused. "So what are you then, Lily Andrews? And what exactly are you doing coming to me with seduction requests?"

Lily sensed an opening and took it. "I'll tell you. But only on the condition we talk about this inside."

"You're assuming I'm interested enough in your answers to bargain. I could just close the door in your face right now." He wasn't even looking at her, his gaze on some people coming up the steps behind her.

Shit. She was losing his attention now. This wasn't going well.

You turn up at his club, requesting he seduce you. In a fucking duffle coat. Of course it wasn't going to go well.

The sharp edge of disappointment sat coldly against her skin. The audition had been like this. She'd danced her heart out, watching helplessly as the director's attention had wandered, trying and trying to get it back. Pushing herself hard. Too hard. Ballet was supposed to look effortless and she'd committed the cardinal sin of making it look like work.

Fuck, she had to do something if she didn't want to fail here too, and something pretty damn drastic.

Behind her she could hear the people approaching the club, guys from the sounds of their voices. Excellent timing.

Kahu's smile wasn't for her as he shifted to greet them.

"All right," Lily said quietly. "If you don't want me, then perhaps someone else will."

She didn't give herself time to think as she turned to face the group of men coming up the steps, because she couldn't afford such a loss of nerve. Instead, she flung open her coat and grabbed the hem of the sweatshirt she wore underneath it. "Hey guys," she said. "What do you think of these?"

As one, the men looked at her.

And Lily jerked up her sweatshirt.

Chapter Two

At first Kahu didn't really understand what she was doing. One minute she'd turned away—with any luck to wait patiently until he had time to call her father, or a taxi at least—the next she had her back to him and the people coming up the stairs suddenly went silent, staring at her in shock. Then they burst into loud cheers.

It didn't take a genius to work out what was going on. The way she was standing, the position of her arms…

"Holy fuck, Lily!" Kahu strode forward, grasped one arm and pulled her around. And sure enough, she had her sweatshirt pulled up to reveal a pair of small but beautifully shaped bare breasts.

Her pale, translucent skin had turned fire red, but along with the embarrassment in her eyes, he also caught a healthy dose of determination. "What?" she demanded, doing nothing whatsoever to cover herself.

Jesus Christ, he hated being manipulated like this.

Kahu reached out and jerked the halves of her coat around her, covering up the snow-white perfection of her skin. "Don't you dare go flashing your tits around like that," he growled, his irritation at the situation morphing into anger. "This is my fucking club not a strip joint."

The men on the steps were still laughing and catcalling. Fuckers.

Lily didn't even seem to notice them. Far from cowed, she stared at him instead. "So are you going to let me in or not? If not, I'm quite happy to stand here with my tits out instead."

Christ, she probably would. There was a stubborn cast to that sulky, pouty mouth of hers, a mulish tension in her delicate jaw. This was a young woman who went out for what she wanted and got it.

Like Anita...

But he didn't want to think about Anita right now. He had more important things to deal with.

Such as one stubborn young girl who was prepared to stand outside on a cold winter's night half-naked, all because she wanted him to seduce her or some such bullshit he couldn't quite get his head around.

Well, he couldn't let either of those things happen, not to Rob's little girl, and clearly he was going to have to do something. The last thing he wanted was for word to get back to Rob that his daughter was outside Kahu's club flaunting herself.

"Hey Kahu," one of the men called to him. "Is she a new member? Because if she isn't, she's got my vote for a membership card."

Something stirred in him, a latent, protective urge he hadn't felt for a very, very long time. Gripping Lily's arm, he tugged her in close, smiling at the pricks standing on the steps gawking at her. "She's the daughter of a friend. So keep your fucking eyes on the ground please, gentlemen."

Without waiting for a response, he turned and stepped back into the foyer, pulling Lily after him and slamming the door behind them.

Once they were inside, he let her go, his annoyance still simmering like a kettle just on the point of boiling. "Come with me," he ordered. "We'll discuss this somewhere quieter."

She said nothing, wrapping her arms tightly around herself. Probably cold, and no wonder.

She did have the most beautiful tits...

Kahu turned on his heel sharply to hide the surprise that came along with the thought. He hadn't thought about sex for six months, not since Anita had died. It was like he'd just lost interest. He hadn't even wanted to jerk off, which was something of a worry since even during his very infrequent dry spells, he'd always at least had a hard-on to relieve. His doctor had told him it was probably just the grief talking and not to worry, so he hadn't. Until tonight.

Tonight, he was pretty fucking worried. Not a glimmer of interest for anyone in six months yet now he was reliving the memory of Lily Andrews's bare breasts? What the hell had gotten into him? Christ, he must be some kind of pervert. She was only twenty, for fuck's sake.

He stalked down the hallway, heading for the private room he liked to use when he had personal friends in the club and wanted somewhere quiet to chat. He'd had a fire lit in there earlier so at least it would be warm, not to mention out of the way if she wanted to try lifting her shirt again.

God in heaven. She'd better bloody not.

Stopping outside the door, Kahu pushed it open. "In here, sweetheart."

She went past him without hesitation, looking around the room curiously before moving over to where the fire burned in the grate.

He'd indulged his taste for a bit of luxury when he'd first had it decorated, with expensive wooden library bookshelves lining the walls, a couple of leather armchairs by the fire, and a long couch covered in worn, dark blue velvet to provide extra seating.

It was a warm, sensual space, his most favorite room in the whole of the club.

"This is nice," Lily said, holding her hands out toward the flames and looking around again. "I thought you might make me wait in the foyer."

Kahu pushed the door shut with a firm click. He remained where he was, standing with the door behind him. This was only going to take five minutes, no need to get comfortable.

"So are you going to tell me what the fuck that was all about or are you going to make me guess?" It came out sounding demanding, but he didn't bother to apologize.

Lily lifted her hands to the hood of her coat and put it back, the light in the room glinting off a tangle of strawberry blonde curls. "Can I have a drink first?"

His patience, already wearing thin, stretched even thinner. "I'm not your servant, sweetheart, and this isn't a hotel. Besides, you're not even old enough to drink." He was being an asshole deliberately, but he didn't care. She had to learn that manipulative little tricks like flashing her breasts just because he'd refused her advances had consequences.

Annoyance crossed her face. "The legal age is eighteen. I'm twenty." She dug into the pocket of her coat and pulled out a blue leather wallet. "I'll even pay you for it."

"Fine. That'll be twenty bucks, please."

She blinked. "Twenty?"

"I've only got scotch and I'm taking extra in damages for that stunt you pulled out there."

A crease appeared between her brows, her gaze searching his. Probably trying to work out whether he was serious or not. He was.

Moving over to a polished, dark oak cabinet, he pulled it open, taking out a bottle of his favorite single malt and a cut crystal tumbler. He poured himself a glass then looked at her expectantly.

"Damages," she said, still frowning. "But I didn't damage—"

"You flashed your tits at my paying customers. This isn't a sex club, love, no matter what the rumors say."

"I didn't see them protesting."

"No, but your father might have something to say about it considering he helps me run this place."

She didn't say anything to that, nibbling on her bottom lip instead. After a moment she opened her wallet, pulled out a twenty-dollar note, then went over to the side table standing next to one of the armchairs and put it down on top.

"There. Twenty dollars," she said. "Can I have my scotch now please?" Then she sat down in the armchair in a fluid, graceful sprawl, tugging down the sweatshirt beneath her coat as she did so, a strip of smooth, white skin flashing

A spark of interest caught him, making him want to stare at that exposed strip of skin. But he smothered the urge. Fuck's sake, if he was staring at twenty-year-old girls, there was clearly no hope for him.

He got out another tumbler, poured some scotch into it then carried it over to where she sat, setting it on the side table and pocketing her twenty-dollar note. Money was money after all.

"Thank you," she said politely as she picked up the glass and sniffed at it. She took a sip, her eyes widening as she tasted the amber liquid. "It's…uh…very nice."

"'It's fifty-year-old Laphroaig so show some damn respect." He dropped into the other armchair. "But I guess that's probably asking a bit much from you."

"You're angry with me," Lily said, taking another sip of her scotch.

"Congratulations on your observational powers. Yes, of course I'm fucking angry with you. I don't like being manipulated. Not by you, not by anyone."

"I didn't manipulate you, I just—"

"Sure, flashing your tits at me wasn't manipulative in the slightest." She flushed. "You wouldn't listen to me."

"I listened to you. You just didn't want to take no for an answer."

Her mouth opened then closed, her gaze dropping away from his, down to her hands where they rested on her thighs, fingers wrapped around crystal tumbler. "Yeah, okay. I'm sorry about that. I only… wanted a chance to explain myself."

Kahu settled back in his chair, stretching his legs out in front of him. Clearly he wasn't going to get rid of her until she'd had time to say her piece, so he may as well get this over and done with right now. "Congratulations. You now have your chance. But make it snappy, little girl. I've got a club to run."

She scowled at the patronizing endearment but he didn't take it back. The more unpleasant he was, the sooner she'd want to leave and the less likely she'd come back.

After a second, she raised her tumbler and drained it, coughing. Then she thumped it heavily back down on the side table. "Okay, so, an explanation." Her voice was full of a kind of grim determination, as if she was forcing herself to speak.

She's nervous.

The realization was unwelcome, stirring as it did the latent, protective urge that had awakened after the incident outside on the steps. She was so young and inevitably naïve. And, now that he thought about it, he really hadn't had very many seduction requests from young women dressed in jeans, sneakers and duffle coats.

Usually they wore a hell of a lot less.

Much to his annoyance, a thread of unfamiliar curiosity wound through him and he found himself watching her. Waiting for her to speak. How fucking irritating. He didn't need to hear Lily Andrews's reasons for wanting a seduction. Especially when he'd heard every tedious story, every single stupid explanation, all the rationalizations for what was essentially a simple, biological need. May as well try to explain why eating and sleeping was necessary. It would make as much sense as why people wanted to fuck. Which was not at all.

You wanted to screw someone because you did. That was it. Everything else was just excuses.

Lily's gaze was serious. Like what she was about to say was terribly important. And it probably was to her. *Everything* was when you were twenty.

"So," she began. "I'm a virgin."

"Oh Christ."

She frowned at him. "What's wrong with that?"

"If you're wanting me to induct you into the gentle arts of lovemaking, you're shit out of luck, sweetheart."

Her frown deepened into a scowl, pale cheekbones flushing. "You don't know what I want. I haven't finished my explanation yet."

"You don't need to finish explaining. I already know what you want. And don't bother protesting because you *do* want me to induct you into the gentle arts of lovemaking."

"But I—"

"You chose me because of my outstanding reputation when it comes to satisfying women."

Her mouth shut with a snap.

"And you think I'd have no problems with screwing you because I fuck anything that moves." Kahu sipped his scotch meditatively. "Am I getting warm?"

She stared at him, her smoky green eyes narrow, jaw jutting obstinately. "Like I said, what's wrong with that?"

He sighed. "If I had a cent for every young woman who came up to me asking for that very same thing, I'd be fucking Croseus. Be original, for God's sake."

"Fine," she said crossly. "How's this then? I'm a dancer and last week I failed an audition. I *never* fail an audition. Never. They said my dancing lacked passion." She paused and he found himself falling silent, waiting for her to go on. "I don't know about passion. So I guess that's why I'm here. I'm hoping you can help me explore what I'm lacking."

Yeah, okay, maybe he hadn't heard this story before. "So you want to sleep with me in order to dance better?"

"That sounds weird, but yeah." She leaned forward, resting her elbows on the arm of her chair. "Passion *is* an experience I'm missing, so maybe if I have it...I can channel it into my dancing." A certain kind of intensity entered her gaze as she stared at him. "Dancing means *everything* to me. I mean, I missed out on a chance to be with the Royal New Zealand Ballet, but there are some auditions happening in Sydney in six weeks. They're by invitation only, so I'm going to send in my CV and hopefully I'll get picked." The light in her eyes was almost fanatical. "I want this audition. I *want* it. And I'm prepared to do anything I can to get it."

"I see." Kahu lifted his glass, took another sip, studying her. He had to admit, that intensity was oddly compelling. Anita had been that way about the piano. She'd been religious with her practice and a complete perfectionist when it came to her performances. Not that there had been many by the time he'd met her, but even in the waning years of her career, she'd still practiced at least two hours a day. "Okay, so you deserve a few points for more originality at least," he continued. "But you still haven't explained why you chose me to be the lucky breaker of your hymen."

"Uh, to be fair, I probably don't have a hymen anymore." She waved a hand. "Dancing is...you know...very athletic."

"Hymen or not, answer the question."

She laced her fingers together. And for the first time, a hint of uncertainty crept into her eyes. "Because...well, I know you. And I trust you." Another hesitation, her gaze flickering away again before coming back to his. "And I want you."

Kahu said nothing to this, merely looking at her from over the rim of his tumbler.

Shit. Why had she said that?

Because it's true? And you want him to know it?

Restlessness filled her. God, she hated sitting still. Pushing herself out of her chair in a sharp, sudden movement, she went over to the fire again, sticking her hands out to the flames, the tips of her fingers tingling.

Yeah, she did want him to know it. At least it probably made more sense than the jumbled up explanation about why she wanted this seduction in the first place. Her feelings about the whole thing were complicated and she barely understood them herself, let alone trying to explain them to another person.

She'd fibbed a little bit about the audition and what the directors had said about her trying too hard. Mainly because she didn't want to talk about the missed years she had to make up for. About how her body, once a finely tuned and well-oiled machine, had failed her four years ago and how it continued to keep failing her.

How some days she hated it.

About how she had to do something to get back the control over it. Because if she couldn't dance, she may as well have let the leukemia take her.

But you didn't. Because fighting is all you know how to do.

Lily stared at the flames, trying not to be so conscious of the man in the armchair behind her. Jesus, she *really* should have shut up.

The silence lengthened.

Lily's restlessness doubled. Abruptly she shoved her hands in the pockets of her coat again and turned around to face him. "Sorry," she said sarcastically. "Did that embarrass you?"

Kahu's dark eyes betrayed nothing. He sat there with his legs outstretched and crossed at the ankles, long fingers cradling the crystal tumbler. Loose and relaxed, as if he didn't have a care in the world. She couldn't seem to drag her gaze from the hollow of his throat, following the line of the necklace cord to where it disappeared under the white cotton of his shirt.

"No," he said after a long moment. "You didn't embarrass me. And I'm flattered, obviously. But, sweetheart, you barely know me." His deep, husky voice had gentled, like he was speaking to a child.

A spike of anger shot through her. "I know enough to want to fuck you. Do I need to know anything else?"

He didn't seem offended. In fact, the bastard only laughed. "I'm supposed to be the one objectifying you, not the other way around."

"Stop being so fucking patronizing."

"Darling, you're twenty years old. Everything I say to you is going to sound patronizing."

He wasn't going to take her seriously, was he? God, she hated being told no. It only made her want to fight harder to get the yes she wanted.

Lily took a couple of steps toward him, stopping short of his feet. She wasn't quite sure what she wanted to do, only that it had to be something drastic. Like she'd done out on the steps of the club.

Her hands went to the sides of her coat and his gaze followed the movement. "What did I say about originality?" he said mildly. "I've had hundreds of women strip in front of me, love. You'll be just one more."

Lily stared at him, caught not by his words but by the tone running beneath them. A genuine world-weariness. Well, Jesus, no wonder, given the reputation he had for cutting a swathe through the female population of Auckland. And some of the male too from all accounts.

He's right. Stripping and being shocking in front of him is not going to get you what you want. Not from someone like him.

She let go the sides of her coat, folded her arms instead. "What can I say to make you change your mind?"

"Nothing."

"Give me a chance to try at least."

"Why should I? You haven't given me a good enough reason to put my long and enduring business relationship with your father at risk by screwing his virgin daughter."

"Dad doesn't have to know."

Kahu rested his head back against the chair, looking at her from underneath his long, ridiculously thick black lashes. "If there's one thing I've learned over the past thirty-eight, nearly thirty-nine years, it's that nothing stays secret for long. And while we're on the subject of years, you do realize that I'm old enough to—"

"Don't say it."

"Be your father."

"And you think I'm being unoriginal. Is that the best excuse you've got?"

He was silent a long moment, the roughly handsome lines of his face giving nothing away. Then he raised the tumbler and drained it before putting it back on the side table with a click. "I don't think getting angry with me is the best idea. That's not going to get you anywhere."

"I'm…not angry."

"Sure you are." Kahu pushed himself out of the chair. "You're pissed I said no."

Lily swallowed as he straightened, aware of how close he was standing all of a sudden. She felt dwarfed. Jesus, she barely came up to his shoulder. She tilted her head back, looking up at him, unfamiliar physical awareness pouring through her.

He was all wide shoulders, broad chest and powerful arms. Not at all like the slender muscularity of the male dancers she'd been used to. Or the male doctors she'd met, not that she counted them since gender didn't matter when you were in hospital.

Do you really know what you're asking for?

The thought crept through her, trailing a thin thread of fear after it. Sex wasn't something she'd thought about in any great depth for years. Not when nausea and weakness and pain had dominated her life for so long.

"Yeah, okay, so I'm pissed," Lily said fiercely, denying the fear. "I don't like people telling me no."

His mouth curved in a faint smile. "I can see that. You must have terrified the people at your audition."

Well, no, not quite. "Which is exactly why I'm standing here."

He studied her for a moment. "Is dancing really that important to you?"

"I don't know, is breathing important to you?"

"Ah. Like that, I see."

"It *is* like that."

Kahu folded his arms, the movement making him seem even bigger somehow. The white cotton had pulled tight across his biceps, the color highlighting the bronze skin of his long, taut forearms. "Lily," he said with that infuriating gentleness. "You can't make me change my mind."

"Would you like me to sit outside your club for the next couple of weeks? Or maybe I'll just call Dad. Tell him you're hitting on me and I don't like it."

A crashing silence fell.

The smile never wavered on Kahu's face, though the look in his eyes became sharp, piercing her like an arrow. "You're not going to do that." His voice remained soft. "You're a better person than that."

Shame crept through her, burning in her cheeks, because again, he was right. It had been an empty threat uttered to regain some control over a situation that was rapidly spinning out of it.

God, she was so sick of feeling powerless.

She wanted to move again, pace around to get rid of the sensation, but she made herself hold her ground. Look him in the eye. "I'm sorry. I shouldn't have said that."

"No, you shouldn't."

"Kahu, please." It wasn't much, but the simplicity of the request was all she had left. "Help me."

Something changed in his expression then, the sharpness fading. "Fuck." He let out a breath, his gaze flickering away. For a long time he was silent, then he said finally, "Okay. I suppose I could."

She blinked, not expecting it. "What? How?"

"Make no mistake, I'm not going to sleep with you. But perhaps I could help you learn a few seduction techniques."

Well, shit. How did that work? She frowned at him. "I'm not sure how that's going to help me. I'm after passion not seduction."

"An audition *is* a seduction. And passion plays a part. For a good seduction to work, you *have* to be passionate. But I'm not talking about physical passion, I'm talking emotional passion. You have to want it and show them you want it. You have to commit wholly to it, seduce them into wanting you instead of anyone else."

You're holding back…

The words of the director were loud in her head. She'd never thought of an audition quite in those terms before but…he had a point. "I guess so. Except… How do I do that? I don't think they'd take too kindly to me taking off my clothes all of a sudden."

"Seduction isn't wholly about sex. It's about appealing to people intellectually as well as physically. Going for their hearts and minds, as well as their bodies. "

She shifted restlessly. "Yeah, I can see that. But… What do you mean by helping me learn a few seduction techniques?"

"I'm a thirty-eight-year-old, jaded and cynical manwhore. I've seen everything. Done everything. And if you can seduce me, Lily Andrews, you can seduce anyone."

"Wait. You mean you want *me* to seduce *you?*"

He was already moving past her, going over to the door. "I don't want you to do anything, love. I'm just saying, if you can make me sit up and take notice, then you'll have those people at the audition eating out of the palm of your hand."

"But…I don't know how to do that."

Kahu paused at the door, turning back to look at her. "Think about it. I've given you a few pointers already."

Lily tightened her folded arms over her thudding heart. "I mean, where? When?"

He was silent a second. "When is your next audition?"

"In six weeks."

"Okay, how about this then? Every Monday night you have exactly one hour in which to try and seduce me. Seven till eight p.m. No touching."

She hadn't expected this, not in the least. But it was…intriguing. A challenge. "But what's the point if you're not going to have sex with me?"

"Sex isn't the point, remember? But hey, feel free to see if you can get me to change my mind." He grinned at her suddenly, a boyish, cocky kind of smile that made him seem a lot younger than he was. "You've got six weeks."

Chapter Three

"Hey, what's up with you?" Eleanor was looking at him strangely, and Kahu realized she'd been waiting for a response from him for a while and he hadn't said a word.

With an effort, he pulled himself together and gave her a practiced smile. "What? Nothing."

"Yes, there is. You've been quiet the whole evening. It's not like you."

Kahu let out a silent breath. He felt strangely flat but then he always felt that way on Thursdays. At least he had since Anita had passed away. Thursdays had been the day he'd visit her, which mainly involved reading her favorite books aloud to her since conversation was impossible. Especially since she hadn't known who he was anymore.

He'd liked those afternoons, sitting in her room that was always drenched in sun. The whole place would be quiet, a kind of hushed silence, as if everyone there was holding its collective breath. He'd found it restful. Anita had used to sit in a chair by the window while he'd had the chair opposite. Sometimes she'd be agitated seeing him, sometimes she'd only stare. When she could still speak, she'd kept asking him who he was, or calling him George, her late husband's name. He'd always reply that he was a friend.

And then he would sit down and read to her and she'd always calm down. Her eyes would close and for a precious twenty minutes or so, she'd look like the woman she'd once been. The woman he'd once loved.

He missed those afternoons.

"Yeah, I'm just tired." He leaned forward, grabbed his glass of wine and took a sip. It wasn't scotch but then it was still only five p.m. Hardly scotch o'clock.

"And you look it." Eleanor, one of his closest friends, narrowed her gray eyes at him. "What's going on?"

Jesus, he'd forgotten what a pain in the butt Thursday night drinks could be. He and the small group of people he'd met during his abortive couple of years of law school, got together every Thursday night in the Ivy Room of the Auckland Club as a catch-up.

Normally it had been the four of them: himself, Eleanor, Victoria and Connor. Then Victoria and Connor had separated, while six months earlier Eleanor had fallen in love with a younger man, and things had changed.

Luc, Eleanor's lover, had joined them on a semi-regular basis, while Victoria and Connor never came together.

Perhaps that's why he felt flat. Too many changes. Not that he didn't like Eleanor's guy. When they'd first got together, Kahu had read him the riot act about never hurting Eleanor otherwise he'd be dead. Luc had told him to fuck off and mind his own business. All good, in other words.

Connor, on the other hand, had gotten way too starchy since he and Victoria had split. He'd once been a relaxed kind of guy, but not anymore. Since he fronted his own law firm and was making a name for himself, it was like he couldn't put a foot wrong or something.

Kahu's antithesis.

"Kahu, come on." Eleanor raised a brow. "This is the second time you've basically ignored me."

"You really want to know?" He wasn't going to tell them about Anita, no one knew she'd died and he didn't want to go into a whole lot of explanations now. "I'm thinking about selling the club."

Eleanor's gaze went wide. "What? Really?"

Across the table, Connor, who'd been talking to Luc, stopped all of a sudden, his sharp, blue eyes coming to Kahu's. "You're kidding me?"

"Nope." Kahu took another sip of his wine. Perhaps he shouldn't have come out with it like that, given his friends a bit of time to adjust or…something. Whatever, it was his club. He could do what he liked with it.

"But…why?" Eleanor asked. "I thought you loved this place?"

He found his gaze caught by Eleanor's hand on the table, her pale fingers laced with Luc's dark, tattooed ones. For some reason the sight of it made something inside him tighten, though he couldn't imagine what that might be.

He didn't want a lover right now. And he certainly had never been all that fussed about love. Been there, done that, got the cracks through his heart to show for it.

"I do," he said, dragging his gaze away from their fingers. "But, you know, we all have to move on at some stage."

"Yeah, but you? Move on from this place? I mean…" She trailed off.

Connor's dark brows twitched. "What are you going to do instead? Buy another bar?"

"Why? Because I haven't got any other qualifications?"

"Exactly." Connor never shied away from the truth. Fucking lawyer that he was. "Not that that will be an issue, of course. You'll get millions from this place, I would think."

Naturally he would also think in terms of money. Connor didn't have a sentimental bone in his body. Then again, neither did Kahu. At least, he never had before.

"Enough to retire on, you think?" Kahu asked him.

Connor looked around, assessing. "Possibly. The market in Auckland isn't hugely buoyant at the moment, but I would think you'd get a few million, especially if you sold it as a going concern."

"It's not happening," Eleanor said flatly. "Because Kahu isn't going to sell it, are you, Kahu?"

"I don't think that's your call to make, Ell," Connor said, his frown making him look even more severe than normal.

"Hey, I spend a large proportion of my time in this place. I think I have a right to at least tell him when he's being a fucking idiot."

Connor opened his mouth to no doubt argue with her when his mobile went off. His frown deepened as he checked the screen. "I have to get this," he said tersely, picking up the phone and answering it with a cold, "Blake here."

As Connor got up from the table and left the bar area for somewhere quieter, Eleanor leaned over toward the man at her side. "Hey honey, want to go get me another drink?"

But Luc wasn't fooled. He shot Kahu a sharp glance before looking back at the woman beside him. "If you want some privacy, *soleil,* you only need to say."

She rolled her eyes, but Kahu was interested to note a flush rising to her cheeks. Eleanor didn't often get flustered, but Luc was the one person who managed to do it to her every single time. And she appeared to love it.

It was good to see her happy. She deserved it so much. He didn't know the details of what had gone on with her awful divorce, only that it had nearly broken her. And he hadn't been able to fix her.

Like you weren't able to fix things with Anita.

Well, that was a fucking stupid thought. Of course he hadn't been able to fix things with Anita. She'd had Huntington's disease and at its onset, had decided to break things off with him. There was nothing he could have done.

But you wanted to stay all the same.

He'd been twenty-five. So young. His whole life ahead of him. Or at least, that's what Anita had told him. Why stay to look after a middle-aged woman through a devastating disease? Better to go and live your life… Then she'd cut him loose.

He'd been so angry at the time. She'd given him so much. A place to live, an education, music, culture, beauty. All the things a poor rent boy from the streets of South Auckland had never even dreamt of, let alone had within reach.

Everything except love, apparently.

You're still angry about that.

No, fuck, he wasn't. He'd gotten over that a long time ago.

Luc got up, bending to give Eleanor a kiss before he headed through the crowded room toward the bar.

As soon as he was out of earshot, Eleanor gave Kahu a severe look. "It's me, Kahu," she said softly. "Come on."

He stared at her, at the lines of her lovely face. At the light in her eyes. A light that hadn't ever been there before. "You're happy, aren't you, Ell?"

She frowned. "What's that got to do with anything?"

"He makes you happy, doesn't he?"

The frown melted away and she smiled. It was breathtaking. "Yes."

A tightness formed in his chest. Fuck, he didn't know why that was. Happiness was always what he'd wanted for her, so the fact that she'd finally found it should make him feel good. And it did, yet there was another emotion threading through that. A darker emotion. Envy, if he was honest with himself. Because really, who wouldn't want to be that happy?

"That's good, Ell. I'm glad," he said.

"Yeah, well, we worked hard for it. Luc's got...certain issues and the past six months haven't been easy. But we're getting through that." Her gaze was direct. "It's not just that Luc gives me what I want, he also gives me what I need. Things I never knew I needed until I met him."

"I can see that. Seems like my advice was good after all, huh?"

Eleanor's smile deepened. "You could say that."

"That's part of why I'm selling." Kahu pushed his glass away. He could tell Eleanor. She deserved an explanation if anyone did. "I need something more. And I don't know what that is yet. But I have a feeling I'm not going to find it here."

The smile on her face faded. "You think I don't see it, Kahu, but I do. I know you're not happy. And I know..." She hesitated. "You haven't been with anyone in a while either, have you?"

He gave a soft laugh at that. "Shit. Since when have you been taking note of my sex life?"

"Since you don't have one. There's a blonde sitting behind me who's just your type, but you haven't even looked at her. Not once. Now that's *really* not like you."

Actually, she was kind of wrong. He *had* looked at her. But only once when the woman had sat down. Yes, she was his type—or had been up until six months ago—yet she hadn't done a thing for him now. Not even a flicker.

Lily did more for you than that.

The thought streaked through his brain, bright as a comet. And he sat there, transfixed for a second by the memory of white skin like vanilla ice cream. So pale against the black denim of her jeans.

Fucking perfect tits…

A thread of sexual desire pulled tight.

No. Shit no. He wrenched his thoughts back to the present. Jesus, he could not start thinking about Lily like that. If he wanted a quick screw, he should be going for the blonde sitting behind Eleanor.

"Perhaps I've decided to be asexual for a while," he said flippantly. "I've tried just about everything else."

She snorted. "Bullshit. There's something else happening with you. And okay, if you don't want to tell me, fine. But if it's bothering you to the extent you're selling the club you love in an attempt to move on, perhaps you should talk to someone about it. Take it from me, pretending something doesn't exist won't help."

He wasn't pretending. He was grieving. Apparently. Hell, perhaps an inappropriate desire toward the daughter of a business associate was all part of the process. It would certainly explain the urge to help Lily that had come out of nowhere the moment she'd said *please*. Especially when what he should have done was to get angry at her blatant manipulation.

But that simple request…fuck, he hadn't been asked like that for years. If ever. Plus she'd been desperate, that much was obvious. And afraid, though of what he didn't know. Any anger he'd felt had melted away at that stage because he knew fear. Had felt it too many times in his own life to ignore hers. So he'd relented and offered to help. Of course it had also been an excellent way to get rid of her. Hell, with any luck she wouldn't even turn up on Monday night.

"Sure," he said. "I know that. But don't worry about me, Ell. I'll be okay." He reached across the table to put a reassuring hand over hers. "I always am."

Lily stood in front of her closet on Monday evening and scanned through the rack of clothes for the fifty-millionth time. What the hell did one wear to seduce a man? The obvious answer was something short, something with a plunging neckline, or something transparent. Preferably all three at the same time.

The problem with a plunging neckline was that she had no cleavage to speak of. Transparent meant her too-thin, bony body might show. But short…well, she could do short. Her legs were probably the only thing she had going for her.

Lily began to reach for her black lace mini dress then stopped.

Be original…

He must see women all the time in short skirts with their tits hanging out. And certainly the little boob-flashing she'd done hadn't seemed to have any effect on him whatsoever.

Seduction isn't about sex…

She pulled a face, staring at the clothes on the rack. Then abruptly she shut the door and turned around, going over to her chest of drawers. Pulling open a drawer, she rummaged around until she'd found what she was looking for: a pair of black leather paneled leggings and a plain black T-shirt. Nothing particularly seductive about the outfit except the leggings showcased the length of her legs rather nicely. And the T-shirt was moderately fitting. She didn't bother with a bra since she mostly never bothered with one anyway.

Dressed, she stood in front of the mirror and scowled at herself. Not overtly seductive and maybe all the black was a touch aggressive, but hey, he'd suggested originality. And she guessed that not many women would have tried seducing him in leggings and a T-shirt before.

Turning, she went and grabbed her duffel coat, because she felt the cold and she'd be damned if she went anywhere without it. Besides, she could always take it off sexily…or something.

Pausing by the mirror, she checked out her hair, debated briefly whether to tie it back then decided against it due to lack of interest in fiddling with it. Her makeup was non-existent but a brief swipe of mascara and some lip balm would do. Again, he was probably used to heavily made-up girls. Which of course meant she wouldn't be.

Satisfied, Lily went out of her bedroom and down the white-carpeted stairs that led down into the ostentatiously grand hallway. Through a set of double doors off the hallway was the lounge, again ostentatious. Large windows looked out onto her father's immaculate rose gardens and rolling green lawn, reminiscent of an English country manor. Except smaller and located in Remuera in New Zealand.

On a low coffee table next to a silver bowl full of freshly cut white roses, was exactly what she'd been looking for. Her father's chess set. It was beautifully carved and expensive—naturally enough since everything of her father's tended to be expensive—which made it perfect.

Appeal to their minds…

She'd seen Kahu playing chess with her father on the odd occasion and had hung around the room, hoping they wouldn't notice, watching him as he played. She'd at first thought it was strange seeing this massively built, Maori guy frowning over a chessboard. But then as she'd watched, she'd noticed how those powerful muscles of his relaxed. How he'd smiled as he and her father had chatted about adult stuff. He'd laughed when her father had beaten him because her father was good at chess. Yet he'd won too at times, treating the win with the same casualness as he'd treated the loss. As if it wasn't winning the game that mattered to him so much as playing it.

Whatever, she'd decided to take the chess set with her and see if he wanted to play. Perhaps they could sit and discuss that adult stuff. And he'd laugh and relax with her. Talk to her.

What about the sex part?

Lily pulled a plastic bag out of the leather satchel she wore and put all the chess pieces into it.

Yeah, the sex part would happen. She'd make it happen. Despite what he said, that was the whole point of the seduction.

But you know what that means, don't you? His hands on you. His mouth on yours...

A weird, cold sensation slithered down her back. She frowned, stuffing the plastic bag full of chess pieces into her satchel. It was almost like fear, which was odd since she wasn't afraid of sex. She knew how it all worked. Sure, her focus on ballet to the exclusion of all else had insulated her and she'd been a late developer anyway. But she wasn't naïve. How could anyone who'd faced down death, who'd had their body intruded on, pierced, poked and prodded, ever be naïve about anything?

She dismissed the feeling. What she *did* know, was that she wanted this. She wanted both to learn how she could win over the directors at her audition *and* win over Kahu. And she was prepared to work to get both.

Lily bent and picked up the board, starting to tuck that into her satchel as well.

"Hey, where are you off to?"

Her head jerked up at the sound of her father's voice and she turned.

He was standing in the lounge doorway, working his fingers underneath his tie, putting his briefcase down as he did so.

"You're home early," she said, feeling vaguely guilty though she didn't really know why. Where she went and who she saw was her own business. And yeah so she may still live at home, but that didn't mean she was a kid. She'd ceased to be a child the moment they'd told her that her chance of recovery was only twenty percent.

"I thought I'd do some work at home." He frowned. "What are you doing with my chessboard?"

"I'm going to play with a friend." The lie came out easily, naturally. Again, strange since there was no reason to lie about the fact that she was going to see Kahu. They were only going to be talking, right? Or at least, she might have been planning more, but that's what his intention had been. "You don't mind, do you?"

"No." Her father loosened his tie finally, undoing the top couple of buttons on his shirt. His frown lifted. "Ah…that's better. " He wandered past her. "Well, have fun."

Typical. He didn't even glance at her. It had been that way ever since she'd recovered. As if her father hadn't been able to deal with the fact that she was well. As if he'd already let her go. She kind of understood it— her mother had died when she was five and the death had hit her father hard—yet at the same time it was painful.

Because she wasn't dead. She was still here.

Jesus, he hadn't even asked her where she was going. *Yeah, Dad. I'm going to see Kahu Winter. With any luck I'll seduce him and he'll fuck me on the couch in his cozy little study.*

She didn't even need to lie about the chessboard. He probably wouldn't have even noticed. *Oh sure, darling. Have a nice time. Tell him I said hello.*

"Do you want to know where I'm going?" she demanded, unable to help herself.

But he only waved a hand at her. "No, no. You're a grown-up now. Don't need to keep tabs on you these days. But if you're home late, don't make too much noise coming in."

As if he wanted to keep tabs on her anyway.

Lily didn't reply as she stalked into the hallway, anger lodged in her chest like a heavy rock wedged in a narrow gulley. But there was no point arguing or getting sarcastic with him. It only slid straight off him anyway.

Pausing beside the hall table, she looked down at the car keys sitting there. The keys to her father's Jag, his pride and joy. He spent more time with that fucking car than he ever did with her, but maybe that was a good thing. If he'd been a more involved father, she probably wouldn't have spent so much time dancing.

Making a decision, she picked up the keys. He wouldn't need the car tonight and even if he did, fuck it. If she was going out to seduce a man, she was going to do it in style.

The drive into town wasn't long, and miracle of miracles she found a parking spot not too far from Kahu's club. Seven p.m. he'd said. One hour. And he'd given her six weeks With any luck she wouldn't need that long. Shit, if she managed to do well tonight, she may not even have to come back next week.

Locking the Jag, Lily walked up the brightly lit sidewalk toward the old, ivy-covered building that was the Auckland Club. The streets were full of evening traffic and people either making their way to dinner or drinks at the central city's restaurants and bars, or heading home after a late one at work.

The club itself looked deserted. The infamous blue door was shut and there was no one outside, the spiked iron railings at the front doing a good intimidation job.

She paused, looking up at the building, nervousness gathering in her gut, the way it sometimes did before a particularly important exam or performance. But stage fright came with the territory as a dancer and she had her own little rituals for dealing with it.

Staring hard at the door, Lily extended one Converse-shod foot and pointed it. Tapped her toes once on the ground. It didn't make the same sound as a block inside a pointe shoe striking a wooden floor, but the movement centered her like a deep breath.

Lifting her chin, she reached forward and knocked hard on the door in front of her. If he didn't answer her, she'd just sit there again until he did. It wasn't like she had anything better to do after all.

Some time passed, the door remaining firmly shut.

Shit.

Lily raised her hand to knock again. And the door suddenly opened.

Kahu stood there, dressed casually in a pair of faded blue jeans and a long-sleeved black shirt, the sleeves rolled up. His feet were bare, his shaggy black hair damp from the shower he must have just had. It made the faint silvering at his temples more noticeable, but that was in no way a bad thing. He was even hotter with it, if that was possible.

"So, Lily," he said in that sexy, husky voice of his. "You're here to seduce me, I presume?"

Chapter Four

He'd love to have said he'd forgotten she was coming, that her turning up on the doorstep of the club was a complete surprise. But no matter how completely he'd given his attention to club business that afternoon, his subconscious continued to hold onto the memory of Lily's visit with the tenacity of an octopus. Prompting him to do ridiculous things like having a shower before her arrival, as if he gave a shit one way or another, and looking at his watch to check the time. As if he was impatient. Or something.

Madness. She was a little girl who needed a few tips to help with her ballet dancing and that was going to be the extent of their interaction. God knew he had better things to be doing with his evening than spending an hour with a barely-out-of-her-teens child-woman talking about seduction.

Yet for all that, he wasn't unhappy to hear the knock on the door when it came. Or when he opened it to find her small, slender figure standing on the doorstep, a large black satchel slung around her shoulders and swathed in that inevitable black duffle coat.

"So, Lily. You're here to seduce me, I presume?"

She gave him a tight smile that betrayed her nervousness. "That's the idea."

"Well, then. Let's get started. You've only got an hour after all."

He showed her into his private sitting room and she headed straight to the fire like she had the time before, holding her pale, long-fingered hands out toward the flames. The hood of her coat was down, strawberry blonde curls cascading over her shoulders in girlish contrast to the severe black of her clothing. Those curls looked…soft.

Soft curls? Jesus.

Irritated with himself, Kahu went to the drinks cabinet and got out two tumblers. "Scotch?"

"Are you going to make me pay for it again?"

He almost smiled at the grumpy note in her voice. "Not this time. It's on the house."

Her mouth pursed. "I shouldn't. I'm driving."

"Then I'll pour you a smaller measure. Alternatively, you don't have to drink it."

Oh yeah, she was nervous all right. He could see it in the tightness of her jaw and around her shoulders, her feet shuffling as if she couldn't keep still. Christ, what did she think he was going to do? Ravish her on the floor or something? Even he wasn't that much of a pervert.

Flames in her hair. Flames on her white skin. His hand, dark against all that smooth whiteness…

Fucking hell.

"You okay?" Lily had her head cocked to one side like a curious bird.

"Yeah," he muttered and shoved the tumbler of scotch at her. He didn't need those kinds of images in his head. Must be his dry-spell screwing with him. Maybe he should be taking himself in hand or picking up someone for some easy, no-strings sex.

On the other hand, it wasn't like he was a teenager. He could control his urges when he wanted to.

He turned and sprawled in his favorite armchair, nursing his scotch and trying to ignore his overactive imagination. "Go on then, sit." He waved toward the other chair.

She colored for some reason. "Oh…uh…yeah."

Putting down her scotch on the table next to the chair, she began to undo the buttons on her coat.

And Kahu tensed. She'd better not be naked under that. Seemed like a weird hope to have about a woman there to seduce him, nevertheless he really hoped she wasn't. It wouldn't exactly be original and he wanted her to have put more thought into it than that.

Why? Don't you want to get rid of her ASAP?

He decided to ignore that particular thought.

Lily shrugged her duffel coat off in a fluid, graceful movement. And, oh, thank God. No nakedness. Only black leather paneled leggings and a tight black T-shirt.

She reached for her satchel, bringing something out of it and he suddenly understood that perhaps she'd put more thought into her outfit that he'd initially realized. Her T-shirt was tight, molding to the small, round breasts beneath it. And unless he was much mistaken, she wasn't wearing a bra.

Shit. Had she done that deliberately?

Kahu averted his gaze—possibly the first time he'd ever done that when he had a pair of perfectly lovely tits to look at—and gritted his teeth. No, she didn't interest him. Not at all.

Lily looked around for a second, chewing on her lip. Then she pushed the table next to her chair so it was sitting closer to his, nudging her tumbler to one side and putting something else down on top of the table. A chessboard.

He frowned at it, aware of surprise uncurling inside him. "Chess?" he asked, to be certain.

Lily didn't look up, taking a plastic bag full of what were indeed chess pieces out of that cavernous satchel of hers and putting them on the board. "Yup," she said, unnecessarily.

"Why?"

She positioned the black queen carefully. "Didn't you say seduction was about appealing to the mind as well as the body?"

So she'd listened. "This is true."

"And I know you and Dad play chess on occasion. You seem to like it."

He didn't know what to say. Yeah, he did like the games of chess he and Rob played. He just hadn't realized Lily had spotted it. "How did you figure that?"

More color tinged her skin, making her freckles stand out. "I watched you."

An uneasy feeling spread through him, though he wasn't sure why. So she'd watched him play chess. Big deal. "You watched me?" he echoed. "Any special reason?"

She fiddled with the positioning of the black king. "Uh...I just found you...interesting. You didn't seem to care whether you won or lost."

No, he never had. Because once you started caring, you made it matter. And nothing could be made to matter. It was easier that way.

Anita mattered. Eleanor matters.

Yeah, but he'd met Eleanor and Anita when everything was new. Before his heart had been dragged on the ground and shredded. Before his self-worth had shattered like expensive crystal.

When you mattered.

Kahu lifted his tumbler and took a large swallow, the scotch burning a pleasant fire on the way down. Jesus, where had these kind of self-pitying thoughts come from? He needed to stop with this kind of maudlin bullshit.

He still wasn't really sure why he found the thought of being observed by Lily so unsettling. Sure, he'd been watched in a sexual way, but not because of how he played chess or…shit, any other way. It made him feel oddly exposed.

Abruptly Lily looked up from the board. "Why don't you care?"

"About winning, you mean?"

"Yeah."

"Because I enjoy playing. The game itself is what matters."

She studied him, her brows drawn together in a puzzled expression strangely reminiscent of Anita in the art galleries she used to take him to. When she'd stare at a picture or a piece of sculpture unable to decide whether it was art or pretention.

Well, he wasn't art or pretention, and this girl wouldn't understand. Weren't ballet dancers driven? Weren't they supposed to be as competitive as top athletes? Winning would *always* matter to someone like her.

"Play, Lily," he said.

She blinked. "Oh…uh…sure." Picking up one black and one white pawn, she held them in her fists and put her hands behind her back. "Right or left?"

"Left."

She took her hands from behind her and opened her palm. Black.

"How appropriate." He gestured with his tumbler. "You start."

She placed the pawns down on the board then studied it for a long moment before making her move.

He leaned over to play, shoving a black pawn ahead two spaces.

Lily shifted in her chair, drawing her endless legs up onto the seat, crossing them like a child. She moved another pawn. "So…" There was an awkward pause. "Um…what star sign are you?"

Kahu looked at her. That could not be her opening conversation. Could it?

"I'm a Sagittarius," she added. "And you are…?"

"Cunnilingus." A stupid and childish answer, but if she was going to start with inanities like star signs then she deserved childish and stupid. And hey, the response had amused several women and got him laid in the past.

She blinked. "Oh." Her gaze returned to the chessboard. "According to the rumors I was thinking fellatio."

It took him a minute to process what she'd said because he really hadn't been expecting it. Then she flicked a glance at him, one eyebrow raised and he suddenly had the oddest urge to laugh. "Well played," he murmured, a smile tugging the corner of his mouth.

She inclined her head graciously and looked away again, but not before he'd caught the flash of a grin.

Hell, she was pleased with herself. It was endearing. "Scorpio," he said, relenting.

"Scorpio, fellatio… In either case we're doomed." She moved another pawn.

Kahu shifted a bishop, threatening the pawn. "So we've done star signs, what are we moving onto next? Favorite color? Likes and dislikes?"

Lily shifted around on the chair. Clearly she was a fidgety kind of girl. "What's wrong with that kind of stuff?"

"Nothing. If you want to fill out profiles on a dating site or take out a personal ad, that is. It's hardly seductive is what I'm saying." He paused. "At least it doesn't seduce *me*. And that's what you're aiming to do, right?"

She frowned at him again, looking frustrated. "So what does seduce you?"

"Impatient, ballerina? I'm not giving away all my secrets just like that. You're going to have to work to get them."

"I'm not a ballerina."

"Maybe not now. But it's only a matter of time, right?"

She focused her attention back down on the board and moved another pawn. "Yes." And it sounded like a vow. "A year maybe in the corps de ballet and then perhaps I'll get to be a soloist."

Kahu took the pawn she'd failed to move out of the way of his bishop. "You're a determined girl."

She scowled as he put the pawn to one side. "I'm not a girl either."

"Sweetheart, I hate to break this to you but you're only twenty. You barely even know you're alive."

And sitting in the armchair cross-legged, tight strawberry curls cascading over her black T-shirt, small and slender, she certainly looked every inch a girl. Part of that was her build, of course, but there was an innocence to her. Though perhaps that was the innocence of youth.

He sat back and took another sip of his scotch, meeting her annoyed gaze.

"You're really quite an arrogant shithead, aren't you?" she said.

It wasn't anything he hadn't heard before. "It's part of my charm."

"Yeah, well, you don't know everything."

"Of course I don't. That's apparently the privilege of the young." He wanted to smile again at the scowl on her face. It was kind of adorable.

Teasing her could become quite addictive if he wasn't careful.

"Oh, so now I'm the one who's being arrogant?" She leaned on the arm of the chair, the light of the fire making the blonde strands in her hair seem like bright gold thread.

He tilted his head. "I didn't say that. I was merely making a comment on the differences in our ages and experiences." She was quite a pretty little thing. And maybe, if she hadn't been eighteen years younger than him and the daughter of a friend, he might have enjoyed a flirtation at least.

But she was both of those things. Alas.

"You say that like you're sixty and I'm ten." She reached out and moved a knight. To the wrong square.

Kahu let out a breath and shifted it to the right one. "Jesus, do you even know how to play this game?"

"Mostly. Don't keep putting me in a box, Kahu."

He kept his attention on the board. There was a confrontational note in her voice that he didn't like. Mainly because it sounded like a challenge to him and he'd always been attracted to challenges. They were like rules. They made him want to break them.

"I'm not putting you in a box. I'm only stating reality."

"That I'm a little girl who doesn't know she's alive?" Again that confrontational note and far more obvious this time.

He moved his queen then looked up. There was an emerald spark of anger in her eyes. A very real anger.

Interesting.

Kahu sat back. "Oh dear. You don't like that particular reality?"

"I know I'm alive," she said, flat and hard. "Do you?"

Perhaps she shouldn't have been so in his face with the question. This was supposed to be a seduction not an interrogation. But still, where the hell did he get off with his "you don't even know you're alive" comments?

Because she fucking knew she was alive. She had the scars and the medical records and the years of fighting against her own body's desire to destroy itself to prove it. So how dare he dismiss that in one fucking sentence?

Of course, he didn't know about any of that, but she didn't care. She was still angry. That world-weary kind of attitude pissed her off so goddamned much she wanted to spit.

So he might have had a shit life. So what? That wasn't the same as having death waiting by your door for three damn years.

Kahu eyed her. "Do I what?"

"Do you know you're alive?"

He shook his tumbler, the ice in it clinking. "I'm still breathing. Still drinking. Therefore, I'm still alive."

"Living is more than breathing and a damn sight more than drinking."

He gave a laugh, but there was nothing of amusement in the dark sound. "Oh the passions of the young."

Anger blossomed inside her. She knew she should keep it locked down, that this really wasn't the time or the place for it, but she couldn't help herself. "Don't," she snapped. "Don't dismiss me with that kind of shitty attitude. Yeah, I get you've got this whole world-weary thing going on. That you've been there, done that. But you know nothing about me, so how about you stop labeling me as though I'm just another silly little girl."

His mouth curved but this time it wasn't the genuine, amused smile she'd gotten unexpectedly not five minutes earlier, the one that had made her feel pleased with herself. This smile was sharp, pointed and completely cynical. "So tell me who you are then, Lily Andrews. How are you different? What makes you so fucking special?"

I nearly died of leukemia. That's how fucking special I am.

She bit down on the words. No, she wasn't going to tell him that. She wanted to leave the whole illness thing out of this, especially when the whole reason she was here was to seduce him.

Sure, tell him about the cancer. Needles and vomit and blood and catheters. That's pretty damn seductive, right?

Lily straightened in her chair, picked up her own tumbler and took a sip of her scotch, resisting the urge to chug it straight down. "All right, I'll tell you then. I've spent the last thirteen years of my life dancing." Even when she was in hospital she was still dancing, in her head. "Ballet is what I live. What I breathe. Right from the moment my mother took me to my first lesson when I was five, that's what I wanted to do. That's *all* I wanted to do."

The cynical smile twisting his mouth had eased and now he was looking at her from beneath his lashes. There was something quite focused about the look, something that made her breath catch.

God, even though she was quite pissed with him, he was so unbearably sexy sitting there with his long legs outstretched and crossed at the ankles. His black shirt unbuttoned at the neck and sleeves rolled up to reveal the long, lean muscles of his forearms and supple wrists. She could see the black ink on his skin, just a glimpse peeking out from underneath his shirt, so insanely hot.

"I hate to have to say this, love," he said after a moment, "but honestly, how does loving ballet make you special? I mean…Jesus…if that's the only thing you're interested in, no wonder you're still a virgin."

The words stung. But she'd already worked out that getting mad about his outrageous statements wasn't going help. Which meant she had to do things a bit differently. Surprise him. In fact, hadn't that been what he'd been trying to tell her before? Be original...

With a conscious effort, Lily relaxed the tension in her shoulders. "You're right," she said mildly. "I'm a fucking awful conversationalist. Would you believe I've never even had a boyfriend?" It was, sadly, true. Not that she was that sad about it. Before she'd gotten sick, a boyfriend seemed like way too much distraction from dancing, and afterwards... Well, afterwards, who wanted a skinny redhead in remission from cancer? And besides, being touched by death changed a person. Stained them. People could sense it and it made them uncomfortable so they avoided you.

"I can believe that," Kahu said, finishing the last of his scotch and setting his tumbler down. "You're also a lousy seductress."

"Gee. Thanks."

"Isn't that why you're here? To learn how not to be a lousy seductress?"

Lily picked up a pawn since it was her turn and put it somewhere that was hopefully threatening. "I am. In which case, if I'm lousy, what does that say about you as a teacher?"

He shifted, leaning over to study the board and she couldn't stop from watching him move. Powerful, muscular, built solid and strong. And yet there was a grace to him she hadn't expected. Like one of those massive, big, predatory cats.

The thought made awareness shiver over her skin.

He'd be able to lift her no problem. Those long fingers would grip her hips, his muscles would flex and she'd be airborne. She'd never want to stop flying...

"I'm not your teacher, ballerina," he said, moving his queen to take her knight in yet another move she hadn't seen coming. "I'm merely here for you to practice your technique on."

She swallowed, the aware, shivery feeling moving lower down inside her as he curled his fingers around the knight and put it to the side of the board. "But how can I practice when I have no technique? Maybe I need a teacher."

He sat back in his chair again, that enigmatic dark gaze of his meeting hers. "Oh come on, Lily. It's not that hard. You have a brain, don't you? I'm sure you can figure it out. I'm only a man and men are relatively simple creatures."

She found herself chewing on her lip again and stopped. "Simple? You?"

"Yeah, pretty much. I like a good scotch. I like good sex. And…" He paused, something glinting in his eyes. "I'm enjoying this chess game rather more than I thought I would."

Warmth crept through her, heating her cheeks. But she didn't want him to know how much the tiny compliment had affected her so she looked once more at the chessboard. "I thought we weren't going to do likes and dislikes?"

He laughed, a shockingly sensual sound. "We weren't. Maybe your technique isn't so lousy after all."

And that felt like another victory.

She leaned her elbow on the arm of her chair, aware of the way the fabric of her T-shirt pulled tight across her breasts, the cotton soft against her sensitive nipples. Weird. She'd never been aware of that kind of thing before. Never thought that just that light brush against her skin could feel…good.

Then she became aware of something else.

He was looking.

Heat prickled all over her in a scalding rush. Her throat closed and her breathing faltered, her heart thumping heavily in her chest. She could feel her nipples tightening into hard little points, becoming even more sensitive.

There was silence in the room, a dense kind of energy gathering between them.

She should probably move, put an arm across her chest. Hide herself. And part of her, the frightened part, wanted to. But she'd been fighting too long to listen to that small, frightened voice, so she stayed where she was. Leaning against her hand with her T-shirt pulled tight, nipples pushing against the fabric. Visible.

And when he raised his gaze from her breasts, she met it, determined not to look away. Wanting to be certain that he was looking at what she thought he was looking at.

A muscle ticked in his jaw and something hot glittered for a second in his night-dark eyes. Something she wanted to reach out and grab onto with every fiber of her being.

Then, without any hurry at all, as if she hadn't just caught him looking at her tits, Kahu looked down at his watch. "Your hour is up. Time to go, ballerina."

Chapter Five

"I have to be honest with you, Kahu. I'm not happy about it."

It was after six thirty and the Ivy Room at the Auckland Club was starting to get crowded with after-work drinkers. Rob had dropped in for a quick business catch-up and they were seated at their usual table by the balcony that overlooked the city.

The man was frowning and looking understandably pissed considering Kahu had just mentioned the fact that he was preparing to sell the club.

"I knew you wouldn't be," he said, leaning his elbows on the table. "So I'm giving you a heads-up in case you want to buy out my share and manage it yourself."

Rob shook his head. "I'm not in any position to be buying you out at the moment. I have other commitments."

Kahu lifted a shoulder. "I'm sorry. But I can't keep the place forever."

"Why not? Anita left it to you for a reason."

He sat back in his chair, his subconscious aware of the noise of the bar, the gentle hum of conversation sounding like the big, happy family he'd never had.

Giving it up would be hard, but he had to get out. Go somewhere different. Recapture whatever it was he'd lost over the years. Whatever it was he'd lost along with Anita.

"I don't want to keep doing this forever, Rob. I need to move on eventually."

The other man sighed. Age had only settled the handsome lines of his face more completely onto him, the atmospheric lighting of the room hiding the worst of the wrinkles and the silver in his blond hair. He looked almost like he had when Kahu had first met him at twenty, when Kahu had been Anita's "new project".

He looks like his daughter.

Oh fuck, he did not need that thought in his head.

"Anita spent years building this place up," Rob said. "I'd hate to see it go to some developer who's only going to knock it down."

"They can't knock it down. The building is classified."

Rob snorted. "You know that means nothing in this town. Not when the only thing they're worrying about is their bottom line."

He wasn't wrong. Selling the Auckland Club would probably mean some kind of demolition. That was just the way it was.

Perhaps you wouldn't mind this place being knocked down. Serve fucking Anita right, wouldn't it?

The anger in the thought was momentarily confusing. Shit, since when had she become *fucking Anita*? He'd never felt that way about her. She'd rescued him from his rent boy existence, she'd given him everything. Why the hell would he be angry with her?

At that point, he felt a touch on his shoulder and then came Mike's whisper in his ear. "Miss Andrews is at the door."

Holy Christ. Of course. It was Monday.

Kahu looked down at the phone on the table and sure enough, it was dead on seven. Lily.

A surge of some emotion he didn't want to look too closely at went through him. Had it really been a week since he'd hustled her out of his study fully ten minutes before the hour was up? And all because she'd caught him staring at her tits.

He couldn't even think why that had disturbed him so much because breasts weren't inherently disturbing. He was a fan of them in fact. Was a fan of most parts of a woman's body. Maybe it was more that he'd determined he wasn't going to view Lily in a sexual way and yet, despite all his good intentions, he hadn't been able to look away. The thin cotton of her T-shirt had pulled tight, molding beautifully to her small curves. Yet it wasn't even so much the shape that had kept his gaze riveted but the way her nipples had hardened as he'd watched. As if he'd touched them. And then he'd glanced up and met her eyes and knew she'd caught him looking. And that she'd liked it.

"Boss? Should I let her in?"

Opposite him, Rob raised a brow. "Problem?"

What would Rob think if he knew his daughter was coming to the Auckland Club for "seduction lessons" from Kahu? The guy didn't have a temper, but Kahu was betting he'd soon find it if he saw Lily standing outside the club.

Perhaps he should send her away, nip this ridiculousness in the bud. Go and find himself a woman, not a girl, to lust over. After all, there were plenty of those to be had. The club itself was full of them.

So you're going to let a twenty-year-old girl get the better of you? Just because she caught you staring at her tits?

Good fucking point. What kind of message would that send if he sent her away? That he couldn't handle himself? That he couldn't handle her? Christ, she wasn't that special.

"Boss?"

"Yeah," Kahu said. "Show her into my study." He looked over at Rob. "Sorry, I'm going to have to go. Got a hot date."

Rob rolled his eyes. "Of course you do. Well, go on then, don't let me stop you."

You might. If you knew who was waiting for me.

Kahu said his goodbyes and made his way out of the Ivy Room. He took his time because he wasn't in that much of a hurry and it wouldn't hurt her to wait.

So it was a full ten minutes after seven when he finally opened the door and stepped into the room.

Lily was standing over by the bookshelves looking at the books. She was in jeans, dark blue skinnies, worn at the knees. Under her ubiquitous duffel coat he could see she wore a soft-looking black sweater—no tight little T-shirts today, thank Christ. She had her hair tied back in a ponytail, a riot of red-blonde curls down her spine.

"You forgot I was coming, right?" She didn't look at him, gazing steadily at the books.

"What makes you say that?"

"Well, you're late. And the room is freezing."

It was true. He hadn't bothered with the fire and since the building was old and the insulation shitty, the room had a chill to it.

Why hadn't he lit the fire?

You know why.

Of course he did. He'd spent the whole week deliberately not thinking about her, minimizing her in his head. Making sure she was in no way special. Making her forgettable.

But when have you ever fought against an attraction?

He never had and that was the problem. And by fighting it, he was already making her different.

She finally turned to him, the delicate lines of her face a feminine echo of her father's. Again, no makeup except for a swipe of mascara and a faint berry stain to her lips. Fresh-faced and so achingly young. "Are we on for tonight or what?"

He wanted to tell her no. That he'd changed his mind and that it would be for the best if she left. But doing that would admit he'd let her get to him, that she was different, and there was no way in hell he was going to grant her that kind of power.

Besides, she'd already set up the chessboard.

"We're on." He moved over to the fire. "Why don't you sit down? I'll get the fire lit."

Lily didn't move from the bookshelf. "You owe me at least twenty minutes."

"I don't owe you anything, love," he said mildly, balling up paper and putting it into the grate, then reaching for some kindling. "These sessions are entirely at my discretion."

"You said an hour."

"And I can change that whenever I want."

"That isn't fair."

"Life's not fair, sweetheart." He arranged the kindling on top of the paper and took out his lighter.

"Jesus, you sound like my father."

And wasn't that a good thing? The more she thought of him as a father the better, right? "You know where the door is if you don't like it." He lit the paper, staying crouched in front of the fire, watching as it caught alight.

There was silence behind him.

He'd been harsh. Too harsh, maybe? Then again, she needed to be reminded who held the power here, that he wasn't to be screwed with. And that if she was going to persist in coming here, it was his rules she had to follow.

"I like your books," she said after a moment.

Kahu put a few larger sticks onto the fire, then rose to his feet and turned.

She'd taken out one of the books and had opened it, looking down. "Oh. Who's Anita?"

A small thread of shock wound through him and he'd taken a step toward her before he could stop himself. Shit, she must have found the copy of *Anna Karenina* Anita had given him. Her favorite book.

He pushed his hands into the pockets of his jeans, trying to get himself to calm the fuck down. What did it matter if she'd found it? It was just a book. And the inscription in the front, *To Kahu, Remember: "There are as many kinds of love as there are hearts." Anita.* Well, that didn't mean anything either.

"You must remember Anita," he said. "Anita Howard."

"Oh yeah, her. She was a really good friend of Dad's." Lily glanced back at him. "She used to come for dinner a lot. And she'd bring you."

The small child sitting at the table, staring at him with wide green eyes. Like she'd never seen a poor Maori boy before. He'd winked at her once, when Rob and Anita had been talking about some exhibition or other, boring shit as he'd thought back then. And the child had seemed just as bored as he'd been.

"Yes. She did."

"Why?" The question was blunt as a hammer-blow. Lily flushed. "Uh...I guess that's kind of personal. Sorry."

Kahu stared at her. Surely she must know about his relationship with Anita? Or at least have guessed? Then again, she'd been a child back then so why would she?

"Anita and I were together." There wasn't a good word for the kind of relationship he'd had with Anita so he didn't try labeling it. "She thought bringing me to dinner with Rob would...teach me a few things." Like how to have a polite discussion that didn't include *fuck* in every sentence.

"You were together?" Her surprise was obvious. "I didn't realize that."

"What did you think then?"

She shrugged. "I dunno. That you were a friend or something."

"Well, I wasn't." He walked over to the couch and held out his hand. "The book, please."

Her gaze had narrowed as he approached, as if she was trying to work something out, but she handed it over without a protest.

The weight of the book was familiar as his fingers closed around it. He'd held it many times over the years, reading aloud to Anita in her sunny room at the rest home. *Anna Karenina* had been all she'd wanted to hear in the final years as lucidity gradually slipped out of her reach.

Happy families are all alike; every unhappy family is unhappy in its own way...

"You're curious, little girl?" He stared at her, irritated for some reason he couldn't fathom. Like she was trespassing on his territory and not even realizing it was his. "Is that what that expression on your face is?"

She must have picked up on his annoyance because her shoulders hunched defensively and she shifted on her feet. "Of course I'm curious. But you don't have to tell me if you don't—"

"I was a rent boy for a few years when I was a teenager. I'd finished with a client when some guy ran past me with a purse. There was a woman on the pavement and she'd been knocked down, so I helped her up. Then I went and found the mugger, beat the shit out of him and got her purse back for her. The woman was Anita."

Lily blinked, her mouth falling open.

His history, greatly condensed. Not all that shocking when told like that, but no doubt the words "rent boy" would conjure up certain images for her. Well, that was okay. The quicker she saw him for what he was, the better it would be for all concerned. His past was what it was and he'd never tried to hide it. Plus, it was his to give and he could give it to anyone he liked.

"She took an interest in me," he went on. "She got me off the streets. She started off being my first female client and ended up being my last."

Lily's mouth closed with a snap. There was a blush on her cheeks for reasons he couldn't be bothered to figure out. Because really, why the hell was *she* blushing? None of this had anything to do with her.

"Oh," she said.

"Curiosity satisfied?"

"Yes."

"Good." He turned and went over to the booze cabinet, putting the book down and getting out the glasses, pouring them each a measure of scotch. Anger burned and he couldn't work out why. He wasn't ashamed of his past. In fact, sometimes he got off on telling people his background. It gave him control over it and he liked having control, that was for damn sure.

Perhaps it was only Anita's name being mentioned and the way it brought back old memories.

Or maybe you just don't want Lily to know those things because she might change her mind about you.

Kahu picked up his tumbler, drained it and poured himself out another measure. The alcohol warmed him, took the edge off the anger. Yeah, and she should change her mind about him. He wasn't a weedy little Remuera boy, with a bank account full of Daddy's money and an old boys network to protect him. He was an ex-prostitute from South Auckland with indiscriminate tastes, who ran an exclusive Auckland club infamous for its risqué parties.

Which meant that if she was looking for a housecat, she shouldn't be searching for one in a lion's den.

He picked up both glasses and stalked over to where she'd set up the chessboard, putting hers down to the side before going back to his chair and throwing himself down into it. "Okay," he said roughly. "Are you ready to play fucking chess or what?"

He was angry. There was a hot glitter in his eyes and his sensual mouth had twisted in that cynical sneer she'd seen the last few times they'd met. She didn't understand what she'd done, but obviously it had something to do with the book she'd pulled down. And with Anita Howard.

Maybe she shouldn't have been poking around in his bookshelves, but then how was she to know that particular book was sensitive? People didn't usually mind others looking at their books in any case. He'd kept her waiting too, so she'd had to do something.

Regardless of her own justifications, however, she'd overstepped somehow and had screwed up the atmosphere between them. Instead of the warm, sensuality of the week before, there was now a chill and hard edges, hardly conducive to seduction.

Refusing to give in to disappointment, Lily slipped off her coat and slung it over the back of the couch. Then she went to her armchair and sat down. She felt cold but tried not to show it, picking up her scotch and taking a healthy swallow in the hope the burn of the alcohol would help. Her head was still spinning from the revelations he'd told her.

A rent boy. She hadn't known his background but she'd wondered about it many times. Wondered why the beautiful, poised Anita kept bringing this rough, uneducated Maori guy around for dinner. In her naivety she'd imagined they were friends or maybe he was her adopted son or…something.

But no. She'd found him on the streets. What kind of life had he had that made him turn to prostitution? A shitty one clearly. Not at all like the world of privilege she'd been brought up in. No, her father didn't pay much attention to her these days but he had once. And at least she had a roof over her head and food to eat. A warm bed to sleep in.

Where had Kahu grown up? How had he ended up doing what he'd done?

Across from her, Kahu sat in his usual sprawling posture, his legs outstretched. He was in jeans again today and a dark purple shirt that contrasted beautifully with his black hair and smooth, brown skin. So gorgeous.

She'd been looking forward to this all week, unable to concentrate on much beyond what her next move would be. It had wreaked havoc with her dancing lessons, her concentration shot to hell. Her teacher had been most unhappy with her. But she'd assured herself it would all be worth it when she got here. Last Monday he'd let slip the fact that he was interested and she was going to build on that.

Except then she'd gotten here and found the room cold and empty, the fire unlit, Kahu not there. Disappointment had gripped her, heavy and…painful.

"What's the matter, ballerina?" he said, his voice low and rough. "Don't like the idea of playing with a guy who used to suck rich men's cocks for money?"

He was being deliberately provocative, she knew that about him now. Perhaps it was how he defended himself, how he kept people at a distance. And maybe that worked on some people. Not her, that was for damn sure.

Lily leaned back in her chair like he was doing and put one leg over the arm of it, her foot dangling. Then she lifted her tumbler of scotch and swirled the liquid around inside it, giving him a considering look over the rim of the glass. "I don't know," she said calmly. "Did you like sucking rich men's cocks?"

Firelight flickered over the hard planes and angles of his face. Heavy, dark brows. Proud, straight nose. Sculpted cheekbones. Lines etched into his skin around his eyes and mouth. Silver in his thick, black hair.

The face of a man who'd seen lots of things. Done lots of things. Who'd experienced the world in all its darkness.

"That depended on the man," he said at last. "And how much they paid me." He paused. "But on the whole, I prefer pussy."

The word jolted her, made her blush. Which was stupid because it wasn't like she hadn't heard it before. It was just the way he said it in that rough, gravelly voice of his, making it sound so dirty. So completely sexual.

"That's good," she said, trying to ignore the catch in her own voice. "It would make this seduction a bit more difficult, seeing as how I don't own a cock."

"It's a moot point regardless of your genitalia, sweetheart. I did say this seduction wasn't going to be about touching, remember?" He tilted his head. "Though of course, if you wanted to pay me, I wouldn't say no."

She forced herself to laugh. "Shit, you should have told me that earlier. I would have brought some cash if I'd have known it would be that easy."

The atmosphere had changed again, not so chilly now but still hard-edged. And there was something dangerous and rough building between them. Something explosive. Like gas in a room, any spark could set it off.

A strange combination of fear and exhilaration settled inside her, chasing away the cold. She made herself hold his gaze, trying to relax and appear as loose and lazy as he did. And failing probably.

"Well," he murmured. "I could always do you an I.O.U."

He was pushing her now and although she could tell herself she was blasé about it, that didn't stop the little shiver of shock from chasing over her skin. Would he really? If she said yes, would he really come over and…

She was suddenly hyperaware of the way she was sitting, with one leg over the arm of her chair. All he'd need to do was lift her other leg over the other arm and she'd be all splayed out, ready for him… A deep, hot ache pulsed between her legs. An ache she'd never been fully conscious of before. She'd always had an awareness of her body but only in terms of how it responded to dance. To the way it moved to music, performed under pressure. A perfectly poised machine that she'd lost control of the day she'd gotten sick.

And now another uncontrollable feeling. Except this time it wasn't bad. Oh no, not bad in any way.

Lily swallowed, her mouth dry. His dark eyes glittered as he stared at her and she could see something hungry in them, that spark of heat she'd seen the week before. The one that had made her want to reach out and grab it.

"Except," she forced out. "You said no touching."

"Ah, that's right, so I did." One side of his mouth curved. "Are you afraid?"

She wanted to move, wanted to shift into a less obvious position but her innate stubbornness wouldn't let her. "No. Why would I be afraid?"

"I don't know, you tell me. I can see it in your eyes, though."

"Maybe it's not fear. Maybe I'm just angry because you're being a dickhead."

"Am I? You're not going to get very far with this seduction, love, if you're afraid of a little sex talk." His smile deepened. "Or maybe it's not sex talk you're afraid of. Maybe you're worried I'm going to come right over there, spread those long legs. Bury my face in that sweet little pussy of yours."

Another hot jolt. More intense this time. Heat flamed in her cheeks and even though she despised herself for it, she looked away, making a pretense of putting her tumbler down on the table beside her chair. "Maybe it's not me who's afraid," she said, trying to keep her voice light. "Maybe you're the one who's worried I might come over there and suck your cock. Why else would you institute a no-touching rule?"

Something fierce flashed over his face then, an emotion she didn't recognize but saw nonetheless. It made her freeze in her chair. Had she got to him? Was it true? Was he really afraid of her doing that?

He lifted his tumbler, drained it and placed it back on the table with a precise click. "I instituted that rule to discourage overenthusiastic virgins. And as much as the thought of a blowjob from an inexperienced girl such as yourself fills me with delight, I'm afraid I'll have to decline."

The fierce expression was gone now, as if it had never been. "Shall we get on with the seductive chess playing or do you have something else you want to do?" He glanced down at his watch. "You don't have a lot of time left."

Prick. Why did he do that? Why did he make her feel all shivery and hot, like he might do *something*? And then the next instant sound bored and like he couldn't wait to get away?

It made her feel powerless. Made her aware that he was the one in the driving seat, not her. Yet another thing like this heavy achy feeling between her legs, the heavy feeling that just wouldn't go away, that she wasn't in control of.

God, how she hated it.

"I guess I could do something," she said, an idea forming in her mind. A crazy and probably downright stupid idea. But shit, if she had the nerve to go through with it, that would wipe that cynical smile straight off his face. "I mean, I know you said no touching each other but…" She steeled herself. "You never said anything about touching ourselves."

The atmosphere gathered tight, the look on his face not changing and yet somehow his features hardening into granite. "You think I haven't had that offer before? Some sweet young thing touching herself up for me? Come on, I thought I said original."

"You think I won't do it?"

"This isn't Truth or Dare, love." That lazy, bored note had entered his voice again. "And I'm not your boyfriend. I mean, really, do you even know how?" He wasn't even looking at her, reaching for his tumbler as he pushed himself out of the chair. "I'll get myself another drink while you make up your mind."

Anger shot up inside her. He didn't care. He really didn't. Wonderful.

This seduction thing was going so great. Perhaps she should quit now while she was ahead.

You're going to give up just like that? Is that it?

No, of course she wasn't. She'd never given up in her life and she wasn't about to start. It was just clear that she would have to form a new strategy.

She stared at him as he stood at the drinks cabinet, pouring himself another measure of scotch. Wide, powerful shoulders, lean waist, strong thighs. Everything a man should be. Making her ache. Burn.

She could spread her legs, undo the zipper of her jeans and touch herself while he watched, that would be easy. But that's exactly what he was expecting her to do, wasn't it? With the subtle challenge in his voice and the cynical look in his eyes. Like he'd already pointed out, he'd had many women do that very same thing, she wouldn't be any different.

But she wanted to be different. She wanted to be the one who surprised him. She wanted to be the one who challenged him.

She wanted to be the one who seduced him so completely he would never remember anyone else.

Lily slid out of the chair and began packing up the chess set.

"What are you doing?"

She didn't look up, sliding the board and the chessmen away into her satchel, before grabbing her coat. "I'm leaving, what does it look like?"

There was a silence.

Lily shrugged her coat on, slinging her satchel over her shoulder and straightening. He was staring at her, his surprise evident.

About fucking time.

"If you think I'm going to sit there touching myself for you while you give me the bored once-over, you're shit out of luck," she said staunchly.

The surprise vanished. He arched a brow. "Does that mean you're giving up this whole seduction farce?"

"No." She began to move toward the door.

"You've still got at least fifteen minutes, Lily."

"Yeah, I know. You can add it to my hour next week." She put her hand on the door handle. "Don't worry, I can show myself out."

He moved toward her, just one step. And she was positive it was involuntary. "Are you sure?"

She smiled, because somehow this wasn't ending as the desperate failure it had started out being. Leaving like this was a victory, she could feel it. Could see it in the frown on his face. "Quite sure. See ya next week, Kahu."

Then she walked out, making sure to close the door very, very quietly.

Chapter Six

Lily turned the bath taps off and stripped. The water looked so goddamned good and despite the two-hour lesson she'd just had, she was already feeling cold.

Fucking cancer. She felt the cold so much more these days. Then again, that was why baths had been invented and she couldn't regret that. In fact, it was almost worth being constantly cold so she had the pleasure of sliding into hot, scented water.

She shivered as she got in, fully submerging her body and lying there, waiting for the heat to penetrate her cold and aching flesh. Because, yeah, she ached too. Her muscles were screaming and her feet hurt like the damned. She'd pushed herself too hard again. Her teacher had been pissed at her and rightly so.

Then again, how else was she supposed to get back into form and compete for a position? She'd missed three years of a career in a hugely competitive industry and the only way to get back to where she was supposed to be was by pushing.

And if you don't...

No, she wasn't going to think about that. It wasn't going to be an option.

She sank lower into the water and put her head back against the tub as the heat eased the soreness in her muscles. Closing her eyes, she let herself float, weightless.

Better to think of something else. Like Kahu and how she was going to shock the pants off him—hopefully.

It had to be something that would stop him talking, since that's how he took charge of the situation. Shocking with his blatant words and his own particular brand of in-your-face honesty. At least that's how he was controlling things between them, not to mention having the added advantage of holding her at a distance.

What she had to do was surprise him. Do something he didn't expect. Get closer in a way that he couldn't fight.

Man, it was a pity she didn't have a girlfriend to talk this over with, but she didn't even have one. She'd lost touch with the girls she'd met via ballet and the couple of friends she'd made in hospital didn't keep in touch, not that she blamed them. It was a reminder of sickness and pain and desperation, and who wanted to revisit that? Good times. Not.

The tension in her muscles uncoiled and she relaxed completely.

Behind her closed lids rose the image of Kahu, sitting in the armchair with that hot, dark look in his eyes. And the rough sensuality of his voice… *Maybe you're worried I'm going to come right over there, spread those long legs. Bury my face in that sweet little pussy of yours…*

That deep, exquisite kind of ache was back as she remembered the moment. How the words had touched something inside of her, something she wasn't expecting. Response. What would he have done if she'd unzipped her jeans in front of him? If she'd put her legs over the arms of that chair? If she'd spread herself out for him?

He'd get up and walk over to you, hungry as a panther. Then he'd drop to his knees and his hands would be on your thighs, pushing them apart. His head would lower and you'd watch as he put his mouth on you…

Lily moved her hand, reaching down between her thighs. Her heartbeat was loud in her ears, her breathing fast.

Do you even know how to do it?

Kahu's taunting voice…

Once, before she'd got sick, she'd discovered how to make herself feel good but it had only ever been as a kind of relaxant. A stress relief. And after that had come the leukemia, destroying her sex drive along with her white blood cells.

She'd never thought her body would be capable of making her feel good again, had totally lost interest in anything remotely sensual or sexy. She only wanted to be well, to be strong, her body once more under her control.

But this feeling… It was good. And hell, she *was* in control. And she *did* know how. It was easy. You just…put your hand there and…

Lily moved her finger experimentally, brushing over her clit, shocked as a white-hot stab of pleasure moved through her. Holy crap. She didn't remember it being intense as that.

Screwing her eyes shut tight, she moved her finger again, the breath escaping her as more pleasure flooded through her aching body. Oh yeah, she knew how to do it all right.

Take that, you bastard. Don't you wish you were here right now?

She imagined him standing at the end of the bath, watching her, that hungry, hot look in his eyes. Unable to touch her but wanting to, so fucking desperate to…

It didn't take long. Another couple of strokes and the orgasm washed over her, brief and blinding. For long moments afterwards she just lay there in the warm water, waiting until her heartbeat slowed and her breathing had returned to normal.

Then she opened her eyes and looked down the length of her body. Long legs and narrow waist. Tiny breasts. There was muscle building but it was slow. Thin and bony, her skin pale, tiny, barely seen marks from biopsies and IV lines and catheters and injections. So many things wrong with it...

And yet it had just given her pleasure. Quite a lot of pleasure.

Oddly proud of herself, Lily pointed her toes, arching her spine, the aftershocks of the orgasm moving through her in little electric jolts. She felt sensual, languid. Pleased with the body that had before caused her so much pain.

So much for Kahu's arrogant "do you even know how" comment.

And even as she thought that, an idea began to form. A daring and no doubt shocking idea. Which made it perfect, especially if she had the guts to go through with it.

Of course you do.

She smiled. Yeah, she did. And with any luck it would shut Kahu Winter up once and for all.

Reaching for her towel, she got out of the tub and dried herself off. Then, wrapping the towel around herself, she grabbed her phone from where she'd left it on the vanity and hit Kahu's number.

It took some time for him to answer and when he did, he didn't sound pleased to hear from her. "What?" he demanded with preamble. "Please tell me you're calling to cancel next Monday."

"Nope." She leaned back against the sink, nervousness gathering inside her. "I'm calling to tell you that you're wrong. I do know how to do it."

"Do what?"

Her cheeks heated but she ignored the embarrassment. "Touch

myself."

There was a silence.

"Lily," Kahu began. "I don't—"

"I imagined you watching me while I gave myself an orgasm and it was really, really good."

Another silence. Longer this time.

Her palms got sweaty as she waited for his response, nerves tying themselves in knots in her gut.

"Jesus," he said at last. "Why the hell are you telling me this?"

"Because if you didn't want to watch me do it, you could listen to me to do it." She took a little breath. "I could right now, if you want."

There was no sound down the other end of the line.

The knots inside of her pulled tight.

He muttered something harsh under his breath and there was a creaking sound, like he was shifting around in a chair. "I'm in the middle of doing the fucking payroll."

"So?" Lily gripped the phone tighter. He hadn't hung up. And there was an added roughness to his voice that hadn't been there earlier. That didn't mean he definitely *wasn't* into it. "This won't take long."

He was silent.

She swallowed. God, what was he waiting for? What the hell else did you say when you wanted someone to have phone sex with you? "I've just had a bath." *Lame, dude.* "And…I'm only wearing a towel."

More silence.

Then his voice, the rough edge in it pronounced. "That's really all you're wearing?"

Oh hell, did that mean he was into this? "Yes."

"Take it off."

Her breath caught. Holy shit. He *was* into this.

Lily's fingers shook as she pulled the towel away from her body, letting it slip onto the floor. Her skin was still flushed from the warmth of the water and the earlier pleasure she'd given herself. But she was ready for more. So much more.

"It's off," she said unsteadily and placed her hand on her stomach. "I'm going to touch myself." Her hand slid down. "I want you to touch yourself too."

Another pause, though this time the quality of the silence was different. As if she'd said something wrong.

"Kahu?"

She heard him let out a breath. "No." A hard note lay beneath the roughness. Like he was angry. "You don't get to tell me what you want, little girl. You don't get to tell me what to do."

"But—"

"You want to seduce me, sweetheart, you're going to have to up your game." This time there was no mistaking it. He *was* angry. "Because you've just made a very bad mistake."

There was more silence and it took her a couple of moments to realize it was because he'd cut the call.

The building heat of desire began to fade, a sick disappointment gathering in her stomach instead.

Shit. She'd fucked up.

You don't get to tell me what you want.

God, she'd said the first thing that had come into her head, hoping he'd be into it, but clearly that had been the wrong move.

Cursing, Lily put the phone down on the vanity and bent to pick up her towel, pulling it around herself, cold again.

Jesus, what more did she have to do?

You could give up.

No. No fucking way. She'd come this far, she wasn't giving up because it was getting far tougher than she'd expected. Surrender wasn't part of her makeup and she wouldn't let it get a toehold now.

She needed a new plan. A better plan.

And just like that, another idea formed. It would be daring, different. It was going to surprise him because, dammit, she'd bet no one else had ever done this one thing for him.

Only her.

The ball slammed hard against the wall, the sound echoing around the squash court.

"Out," Connor said as he bent to pick the ball up.

Kahu shrugged. He didn't much care since the weekly squash games he had with Connor weren't about competition—at least not on his end—but about exercise and spending time with a friend. Connor, though, was not only a stickler for the rules but a competitive bastard and was always in a fine mood when he was winning. As he was now.

"You want to keep going?" Connor tossed the ball in his palm, grinning.

Cocky prick. "Sure." Kahu tightened his grip on his racquet. Squash wasn't his game but he rather enjoyed the conversations he had with Connor, not to mention the beer they always went for afterwards.

Connor slammed out another serve that had Kahu reaching hard to respond to. He missed. Again.

"Your form is sloppy," Connor pointed out helpfully. "Got something on your mind?"

Only a woman who was getting under his skin in a way no woman had done since Anita. And yeah, he was pissed off about it.

She'd walked out on him at their last meeting and then there had been that fucking phone call where she'd told him all about how she'd touched herself while thinking of him. Which hardly made the situation easier.

Last Monday he'd gotten angry, mainly with himself and his confused feelings about her, and the way she'd brought up Anita. Making him feel like he cared about her opinion of him, and he didn't care. At all.

Which you then proceeded to prove by being a prick to her.

Putting her in her place with rough, blunt words. Distancing her. Not that she'd let him get away with it completely, oh no. Then had come that phone call, where she'd put thoughts into his head, of her naked in the bath, her hands between her thighs…

He'd gotten hard. Told her to take that damn towel off. And he probably would have gone further, too, if she hadn't demanded more. Hadn't told him what to do. Hadn't kept pushing.

Kahu turned abruptly away from Connor and strode over to the edge of the squash court where he'd left his water bottle. Stooping, he picked it up, covering his annoyance by taking a long swig.

That phone call had been such an obvious move and he'd been stupid to get sucked into it.

She's been doing so well up till now.

He took another swig, the cool water sliding down his throat. It was true. She had been doing well. Surprising him at every turn. And even the Monday just gone, she'd still managed to surprise him. By bringing up Anita. By not batting an eyelid when he'd told her about his past. By calling him out on his motivations for dirty talking.

When he'd fully expected her to answer his challenge and touch herself in front of him.

But she hadn't. She'd left then turned the tables on him with phone sex instead.

"Hey," Connor said from behind him. "What's up? You're distracted."

Lowering his water bottle, Kahu wiped a hand over his face. "Just thinking about the club."

"Having second thoughts about selling it?"

"Maybe." He let out a breath. "Have you ever been tempted by something you know you shouldn't have?"

Connor's intense blue eyes gave him an enigmatic look. "That doesn't sound good."

"It isn't. Which is why I asked you that question."

"The fact that you've been tempted was reason enough for the comment," Connor said dryly. "You usually don't bother with temptation. You usually just take and fuck everything else."

"This is a special case."

"Clearly." Connor bent to drop his racquet and pick up his towel, wiping his forehead. "I suspect you already know my answer. You ignore the temptation. It'll stop after a while. Temptation soon ceases to become tempting if you wait long enough."

A typical Connor answer. Nevertheless, he knew the guy was right—unfortunately.

You weren't supposed to even be tempted.

No use denying it, though. Or at least, he couldn't say that Lily Andrews did absolutely nothing for him. And the problem was the more he saw her, the more she got under his skin. Which made the answer to that problem simple.

Living in Sin

He had to stop these visits right now. If it had been purely physical he could have handled it. But it wasn't. She got to him on another level and that disturbed him more than anything else. Maybe it was because she surprised him and continued to do so, or maybe it was her sheer unguarded honesty. Maybe it had more to do with the stubbornness of her will. Whatever it was, he had to stop it. Because he knew how vulnerable you were at that age, no matter what front you put up. Hell, he'd been twenty when Anita had come blazing into his life and look what had happened then?

She took advantage of you. That's why you're having difficulties now.

"Or is that not what you want to hear?"

Kahu blinked, realizing Connor was staring at him. Yeah, well, Anita had taken advantage of him, no denying that. But he'd been fully aware of it at the time. And had wanted it. And, shit, look at everything she'd given him? "No," he said and grinned. "That's exactly what I wanted to hear."

"Excellent. Can I ask what this particular temptation is?"

"Can I ask how you and Victoria are getting on?"

Instantly Connor's good mood vanished, his straight, dark brows arrowing down.

Kahu lifted a shoulder. "There's your answer then."

The other man looked down at the towel he was holding, now twisted between his hands. "She's mentioned divorce."

"Jesus." He really didn't know what else to say. Connor and Victoria had always seemed like a solid couple until...whatever it was that had broken them apart had happened. Neither of them had told either him or Eleanor what the difficulty had been, which made offering advice somewhat problematic. "I'm sorry, mate. Is she serious?"

87

"Yes." The towel twisted between Connor's strong hands.

Kahu shook his head. He may not know what had split them up, but one thing he was sure of, Connor was still in love with his wife. "Then you'd better make sure to change her mind. Come on." He put a hand on the other guy's shoulder. "Let's go get that beer."

Friday, Kahu sent Lily a text. *No more Monday nights. I think it's best for both of us if we stop this now.*

He got a response pretty much instantly: *Why not? Scared I'm going to win?*

A win meaning him being seduced presumably.

He leaned his elbows on the dark wood of the bar in the Ivy Room and stared at the screen on his phone. It was late afternoon, the bar closed after the lunch crowd and in the process of being cleaned up for a busy Friday night.

Don't be childish, he texted back. *And I'm not arguing with you. This is my decision.*

A couple of seconds passed and he continued to stare at the phone because if he knew anything about Lily it was that she wouldn't leave it at that. And sure enough, a moment later, the screen lit up with a call.

Briefly he debated ignoring it. But then she deserved more than that kind of response, didn't she?

Sighing, he picked the phone up and hit answer. "Like I said, it's my decision," he said before she could speak.

"Okay."

Which he was *not* expecting. "Okay?"

"Yeah, okay."

Why was he so disappointed? Why did the fact that she didn't even protest make him feel shitty? "Oh," he said, words deserting him in a way they very rarely did. "That's…settled then."

"But give me one more Monday."

He closed his eyes as the disappointed feeling was replaced by something else. Something hotter. Fuck. "Why?"

"You said this was supposed to help with my audition. And I have one more thing I want to try."

Yes. Let her. Just one more time. What could it hurt? You're not going to touch her, you know that. And you did promise to help.

Again, fuck. He had promised. He just…had a feeling that it wasn't going to end well for either of them.

"Please, Kahu? This coming Monday and that'll be it." Her husky little voice sounded perfectly calm and certain. No emotional blackmail going on there.

How could he refuse?

You don't want to refuse.

"All right," he said reluctantly. "This Monday is the last time."

There was a small pause, as if she was steeling herself to ask a question. But in the end, all she said was, "Fine. I'll see you then." Then she hung up.

Slowly, he lowered the phone and set it back down on the bar. Probably a bad decision to say yes. But what could she do in the space of an hour that she hadn't managed over the previous two Mondays or on the phone? Anything overtly sexual wouldn't work and if she tried anything emotional, he'd just boot her out.

It would be fine. Nothing would go wrong.

But as the rest of the weekend passed, he found himself getting more and more tense. He tried to immerse himself in doing the accounts on Saturday, spending the evening in the Ivy Room managing the usual Saturday night madness.

Sunday was cleaning up after the night before then going over to Eleanor's for dinner with her and Luc.

Unlike Connor, neither of them noticed his distraction, for which he was profoundly grateful.

Monday, he sat in his office, going through his emails and liaising with the real estate agents who were all desperate to get their hands on the club. Prime property, they said. Go for millions, they said. He screwed around with them again because it amused him and because doing that was easier than thinking about what plans Lily had for the night.

Christ, the mental space she was starting to take up in his head was just goddamned ridiculous and he resented it big time.

As the evening and seven o'clock approached, he went into the study and lit the fire. He didn't want her getting cold like last time. He also didn't ask himself why that mattered. Then he got caught up with a few original club members who'd come in for a drink, missing the moment she actually arrived.

He was on the point of excusing himself when Mike gave him a nod from the door then jerked his head in the direction of the study.

Kahu ignored the twist of excitement that gripped him, smiling at the people he was with before making an exit.

Striding down the hallway toward the study, he tried to also ignore the anticipation that had merged with the excitement, creating a mix of something volatile he couldn't even name. What the hell was wrong with him that the thought of a meeting with a twenty-year-old girl was making him feel this way?

He was a sick fuck.

Turning the door handle, he stepped into the study.

The room was warm this time, the fire a muted glow in the hearth.

Lily was standing in the middle of the room swathed in her duffel coat again, her hands in the pockets, looking strangely tense. She wasn't wearing jeans or leggings this time, her bare legs showing pale beneath the coat. Except…she had ballet shoes on her feet, pink silky ribbons crisscrossing around her ankles. Her hair was neatly gathered into a red-gold bun on the back of her head, not a curl out of place. And she was wearing makeup, her lashes heavily mascaraed and circled with black eyeliner. She looked like she was about to step out onto the stage.

"Sit down." Lily took a hand out of her pocket and gestured awkwardly at his usual chair. "I poured out the scotch. I hope you don't mind."

"No." Slowly, he walked over to the chair and rested his hands on the back of it. "What's going on? What's with the shoes and the makeup?"

She shifted on her feet, restless and nervous looking, then stopped, her shoulders hunching. "Like I said, I need help with my audition. And since you haven't seen me dance yet…"

Lily. Dancing. His heartbeat sped up for no goddamned reason that he could see. "I'm not a dancer or whatever. I won't be able to offer you any advice, if that's what you're after."

"I know that. But if nothing else, it'll be good practice before the audition. I need an audience."

He sighed and came around the side of the chair, dropping down into it. "Fine." There wasn't any harm in it and besides he could admit to himself he was curious. "Dance then."

She turned away, going over to the side table where a couple of portable speakers were sitting, an MP3 player plugged into them. A tumbler sat next to the speakers. An empty tumbler.

Kahu frowned. Jesus, she must have been nervous if she'd had her scotch already. Did she normally get stage fright? In front of one person?

She bent over the MP3 player and pressed a button. Then she straightened and began undoing the buttons of her coat. She didn't look at him as she did so but it wasn't until she'd taken it off that he realized why.

She wore nothing underneath it.

Shock held him motionless as she shrugged off the coat, tossing it onto the couch before coming to stand in the middle of the room, her arms held down in a gracefully curved circle in front of her.

Fucking Jesus Christ. She was completely and utterly naked.

Countless women had taken their clothes off for him. More than a few had even danced naked for him. Shit, he'd had his share of lap dances and had watched strippers pole dance. He'd even gone to a couple of ballets Anita had dragged him to.

But this… This was different. This didn't feel sexual anymore. Fuck, he didn't know. He only knew he couldn't take his eyes off her.

She was slender yet leanly muscled, her legs long and athletic. Her skin so pale she looked like she'd been carved out of porcelain or alabaster. And yet there was color to her. The pink tips of her small, high breasts. The neat little thatch of red-gold curls between her thighs…

Music filled the room, sounded like Mozart. Lily rose up onto her toes, lifting her arms. Then she lifted one leg straight out in front of her, balancing on the tip of one foot effortlessly before opening her arms out and sweeping her leg around behind her.

Kahu couldn't breathe.

She moved gracefully, weightlessly, like she was about to escape earth's gravity and lift into the sky. Spinning on one toe before taking a couple of steps forward, a small leap then lifting her arms up to the sky and arching back. A wild, sensual creature...

If the dance had been entirely about sex he wouldn't have been affected. Not in the slightest. But it wasn't. The firelight moved over her skin, highlighting the strength of her supple body, the soft curves of those beautiful little tits, catching the gold in the curls protecting her pussy. And yet it wasn't a display of sex. It was a display of strength.

Christ, he could feel himself getting hard and he knew he should get up and leave. Take himself away before this got out of hand. But he couldn't walk out in the middle of her performance. It would ruin it.

She was standing in front of him on her toes, her chin lifted. One arm curved above her head, the other outstretched in front of her as if she was reaching for him.

She was blushing furiously but met his gaze without flinching. So proud. So strong. He almost lifted his hand to touch her and then the music changed and she spun away, whirling around and around in a series of perfectly controlled pirouettes.

Now. Fucking now. He should get up and leave.

But still he sat, dry-mouthed and hard, watching her as she danced for him. Naked and vulnerable and yet so damn strong.

Her back arched, her arms lifting, one leg straight up behind her, her body in a gentle curve. Her nipples had hardened into tight little points. And he could see...fucking hell.

He closed his eyes, trying to get control of his breathing. Slickness between her thighs. Hot pink flesh.

Kahu reached for his scotch and knocked it back, relishing the burn. Hoping it would cancel the sting of desire that slowly and inexorably crept through him.

Again Lily came closer to where he was sitting. The fire had made the room hot, a drop of sweat sliding down between her breasts, her skin deeply flushed from exertion.

He had to get out. He *had* to.

She stood there, legs apart, up on her toes, her arms above her head, looking down at him, proud as a queen.

And he didn't know what came over him but he couldn't stay still. Couldn't be at the mercy of this inappropriate desire or watch her flaunting it in front of him a second longer.

He put his arms on the chair and pushed himself up in a sudden rush of movement.

She didn't flinch, almost as if she expected it of him.

And for a second their gazes locked. She, tall and proud, naked and strong. He, fully dressed and breathing fast, his cock hard. Consumed by a hunger he didn't realize was still possible to feel.

Electricity crackled between them, tension filling the air, a complicated mix of frustration and desire and anger. He could smell her, clean, feminine sweat and flowers. A hint of musk. Her skin glistened in the firelight, her pulse beating fast at her throat.

The music continued to play and before he could move, she'd turned away, taking a couple of precise steps before she kicked one leg out in front of her, another impossible balance on her toes, holding the position before abruptly arching back, kicking even higher, then folding all her limbs up in a graceful fall to the floor.

The music ended.

Silence echoed around them.

He felt like he'd been hit over the head, his ears still ringing with the blow.

Lily moved, shifting from the floor and getting to her feet. The green of her eyes was dark and shadowed, the glitter on her lids from her eye makeup sparkling. Her mouth, full and pouty, was slightly open.

She didn't say anything, going over to her chair and shifting it so it was angled more toward his. Then she turned and sat down, her hands on the arms, her legs outstretched in front of her, her chin lifted and her gaze confronting. Sweat glistened on her body, her breasts rising and falling in time with her quickened breathing.

"So?" she asked, her voice only a little ragged. "How did I do?"

Chapter Seven

Every muscle in her body felt tense, her fingers digging into the arm of the chair, her thighs quivering. But not because she was tired. No, shit, she felt the opposite of tired, all keyed up and humming with adrenaline instead. Like she wanted to keep moving, keep dancing. Break out of her skin. Do *something*.

There was so much energy in the air. In her. She'd never felt that way dancing before. Always her head had been far too much about getting the perfect line, the perfect form, the perfect timing. Making sure her body was doing everything it was supposed to do.

But not tonight.

Oh, she'd felt fucking nervous as hell when she'd taken her coat off and the music had started. And she'd stood there naked in front of him. But then she'd seen the look on his face, the shock. And afterwards… No mistaking the hunger. The desire.

In that moment she'd forgotten about the perfect form, the perfect line. She'd even forgotten about timing. She watched him watch her, letting the music take her where it would, letting her body move as it wanted to. And the freer she'd become, the more intense the look on his face had gotten, the hard ridge in his jeans unmistakable.

He'd followed every move she made as if he'd never seen anything like her before.

And he wouldn't have, would he? She'd bet her life on the fact that no one had ever danced ballet, naked, in front of him before.

Now it was his turn to stand in front of her. And although he was clothed, there was a nakedness in his expression. In the fierce light in his eyes and the way his hands curled into fists at his sides. In the intensity that vibrated off him.

He was motionless but she could feel the energy... God, it was coming from him.

Her breath caught, excitement shivering through her. Well, she'd wanted that jaded, cynical look off his face and it was gone. Completely. And it made her feel so powerful. Like she could do anything.

"You did good," Kahu said, his voice even rougher and more frayed-sounding than normal. "And now you can spread your legs for me, ballerina."

A hot spike of arousal surged through her, along with a healthy dose of shock.

Why are you shocked? Didn't you want him to do something? Wasn't that the whole point of the naked dancing?

Sure, but imagination was one thing. Reality was different.

Reality was, in actual fact, way hotter.

Lily didn't move, wanting to push him, though she didn't quite understand why. "Oh really. And why should I do that?"

"Because I asked you to. Because it's what *I* want." His tone was mild, at odds with the ferocity on his face. "Do as you're told."

Oh, that shouldn't be quite as sexy as it was. It really shouldn't. But he was standing there with all that energy pouring off him, an intense, sexual energy that held her absolutely riveted. That made her want to do exactly what he'd said.

So she did. Lifting one foot then the other over the arms of the chair, so she was splayed out for him. An incredibly vulnerable, exposing position.

Her heart was racing and she felt so hot, her skin on fire. Like she'd never be cold again. And she ached and ached and ached.

Kahu's attention shifted down between her legs and she almost gasped, her fingers digging into the fabric of the chair. He hadn't even touched her and already she was trembling.

The fire was behind him, the expression on his face shadowed. But the glitter in his eyes was unmistakable. He was angry. No, he was furious.

Except when he spoke it was in that same, mild tone. "Like you said last week, there aren't any rules about touching yourself. So go on. Do it. Show me how you make yourself come like you told me you could, Lily darling."

She took a ragged breath. "Why are you so angry? What did I do?"

"I don't like being manipulated."

"I didn't—"

"Put your hand between your legs, ballerina, and stop arguing with me. If you're going to make me burn then you'd better be prepared for some payback."

Make me burn…

The air rushed out of her. Okay, so she could kind of see why he'd felt manipulated. She'd come in here all naked and stuff, prepared to knock his socks off, but not for him, only for herself. Because she was competitive and she had her pride. Because failure wasn't an option.

So you'd better take the consequences, hadn't you?

"W-what if I don't want to?"

His intent dark gaze didn't move from hers. "Then you know where the door is."

So, she could leave. But then that would mean backing down. That would mean admitting she was scared, that she wasn't ready. Failure.

Fuck that. This was like the moment in the bath, where she'd made herself come imagining him watching her, watching but unable to touch...

Lily put her hand on her stomach and slid her fingers down between her thighs, muscles instinctively tightening as she did so, another wave of heat washing over her.

"Put your thumb on your clit," Kahu ordered. "Stroke yourself."

She swallowed, dizzy at the sudden rush of pleasure as she moved her thumb like he said, brushing over the sensitive flesh between her legs. And again. And again. She let out a ragged, gasping breath, shifting restlessly on the seat.

The fire leapt behind him, light flickering over his face. "Slow down and keep it slow."

No, God, she didn't want it slow. But there was something so compelling about his voice, about what he was telling her to do that she obeyed without thought, her movements becoming languid, tantalizing. Small, aching circles.

She closed her eyes, pleasure gathering inside her in a tight, hot ball.

"Eyes on me, ballerina."

It didn't even cross her mind this time to disobey, lifting her lids to find him watching her. Hot. Dark. So hungry... The air escaped her lungs, shivers whispering over her skin.

"Fingers in your pussy," he said softly. "Keep that thumb on your clit. Nice and slow, Lily. I want to see you panting for it. I want to see you desperate."

Oh Jesus. Why was this so fucking hot? Why was she on the edge of orgasm so quickly already?

She didn't even think about not doing it, reaching lower, easing one finger into her sex. Her flesh felt hot, slick, tight around her finger, her thighs trembling.

"Deeper." Kahu's voice sounded much rougher now, his jaw tight, the expression on his face like a man starving.

She slid her finger in farther, her hips lifting instinctively. A gasp escaped her dry throat. God, this was…intense. And so, so good. The pleasure that was rushing through her was inexorable. Unstoppable.

Moving her hand, Lily began to pant, her gaze fixed to his. Watching the effect she was having on him, seeing the darkness move in his eyes.

It was addictive, this kind of power. A power she'd never thought or even expected to have. The power of her passion, her sexuality. Her body working as it should, giving her so much pleasure. And all completely under her control, all totally driven by her…

Until Kahu stepped up to the chair and leaned over her, shocking her into immobility. He put one palm on the back of the chair near her head and without saying a word, reached down and gripped her wrist, pulling her hand away from her body.

The touch of his skin on hers was like a lightning rod, conducting raw energy straight through her. She gasped aloud, freezing in the chair, trembling all over, her body screaming.

Don't stop. Don't stop, please.

Perhaps he wasn't going to stop. Perhaps he was going to put his own hand down there, touch her aching flesh. Slide his finger inside her, make her come so hard.

"Kahu," she whispered, helplessly.

He was so close, the heat from his body against her bare skin hotter than any fire. And he smelled like laundry fresh off the line, clean and hot in the sun, with a faint spicy scent. Tea tree or cedar or something.

All she could think was yes, fucking finally. He was going to touch her. He was going to do what she'd been wanting him to do for so long.

But he didn't.

He lifted her hand, his tar-black gaze on hers.

Then he put the fingers that had been between her legs into his mouth.

Heat exploded against her skin, the eroticism of it making her gasp aloud again. "Oh...Jesus..."

Gripping her wrist tightly, he sucked at her fingers then licked them, watching her all the while. And when he finally drew them out of his mouth, he nipped the tips, sending electric shocks echoing down her nerve endings.

She was shaking.

He let her go, stepping back, taking all his heat and that warm, sensual spicy scent with him. "Remember this when you burn for me, ballerina," he murmured. "Because it's all you're going to get."

Then he turned and stalked out of the room, the door closing with a sharp click behind him. And it was like he'd taken all the heat with him, leaving her shivering and cold and aching in the chair.

Alone.

Chapter Eight

Kahu arranged the roses he'd brought—half a dozen, long-stemmed, red—on the ground before the black granite headstone. Then he stepped back and stood there for a moment, staring at Anita's grave.

In memory of Anita Howard. Always loved.

She'd had no one in the end. No family. Her friends all having left her after she'd gotten sick and at her own request.

He'd been the one who'd given those words to the masons who'd made her headstone. And he'd been the one who'd tidied up her affairs after she'd gone. Who'd visited her every Thursday for the past five years, reading to her from a book she'd long since ceased to understand.

And in the end, when she'd died, it was her husband she'd wanted to be buried beside. Her long dead husband, the love of her life.

Not you, in other words.

That wasn't anything he didn't know. He was her project, her pet and he'd understood that right from the start. Their relationship was a transaction: he gave her sex, she gave him everything else.

Except of course the thing he'd wanted most—her love.

Because the sad fact was that even though he'd known exactly what he was getting himself into when he'd first accepted her invitation to come home with her, even though she'd told him straight up what their relationship was all about, he'd fallen in love with her anyway.

He pulled the black captain's coat he wore more tightly around him, turning the collar up as the wind whipped across the tiny Auckland cemetery. Then he clasped his hands in front of him. He didn't think much of God, but he believed in the comforting power of words so he whispered a prayer in Maori his mother had taught him years ago—his customary greeting to Anita—then stood there for a while wondering what else to say.

Thursdays was Anita-visiting day and normally, he didn't have any problem with thinking of things to tell her about. A précis of his week. A rundown of how the club was going. Sometimes a retelling of his latest sexual conquest, which she'd always enjoyed in life. Except he didn't have any recent sexual conquests.

You fucking liar.

His jaw tightened. The sun came out from behind a cloud, picking up the quartz sparkles in the granite headstone.

Of course he had a recent conquest. Or rather, he was the one who'd been conquered. By a fucking twenty-year-old ballet dancer in pink pointe shoes.

The anger that had been there since Monday night, flared once more into life.

He could see her in his head, lithe body sheened in sweat as she'd danced around the room for him. Light, graceful. Beautiful. She'd made him burn, made him ache and he'd been so damn furious with her for it.

He'd tried at least to get some of the power back by making her experience that same burn, that same ache. But then she'd rendered him helpless by doing everything he'd told her to.

Christ, he'd been so hard looking at her, the vicious desire tightening at the sight of her spread thighs, her fingers at her pussy, her face flushed, eyes dark with passion. Watching him.

How he'd managed to stay in control enough not to pull her from that chair, push her onto the floor and bury himself inside of her, he'd never know. That he'd been unable to keep from touching her at all was pretty fucking bad enough.

Those long, pale fingers had tasted of salt, with a tart sweetness that hit him like a punch to the gut. Making his mouth water for more. He'd so very nearly put his own hand between her thighs, touched that slick pink flesh for himself. But he'd remembered his promise at the last moment. Remembered he wasn't supposed to be touching.

Remembered that she was someone he wasn't supposed to want.

His hands tightened around each other, an involuntary movement.

Maybe she hadn't meant to manipulate him with sex to get what she wanted, but it sure fucking felt like it.

Like Anita, right?

No, it had been different with Anita. She'd always been straight-up. She'd always given him choices. But Lily hadn't. She'd wanted a victory, wanted to seduce him regardless of his feelings on the subject.

She'd forced him into a situation where he'd broken his no-touching promise.

Hey, no one forced you to tell her to touch herself. No one made you put her fingers in your mouth.

Kahu growled. All that was true and blaming Lily for his own weakness was unfair. But that didn't make him feel any less manipulated. Or less angry.

Or less hot for her than he already was.

After he'd left her sitting in the study, he'd gone straight upstairs and relieved himself of the hard-on that had been driving him mad, jerking off with Lily's taste in his mouth and visions of her naked body in his head. First time he'd done it in months and it had to be to images of the one woman he shouldn't be having these thoughts about.

In fact, even thinking about it now was making him hard all over again.

Angry, Kahu turned from the grave, thrusting his hands into the pockets of his coat. One thing was certain; he was going to do exactly what Connor had advised and that was to steer clear of temptation. No more Mondays. And as to sex, he'd see if he could get his head back in the game with a trawl around the club. Or maybe dusting off his languishing address book.

He was on his way back to the carpark when his phone buzzed in his pocket. Pausing, he hauled it out and checked the screen then hit answer. "Hey, Rob. What's up?"

"I've been thinking, Kahu," the older man said. "I want to discuss the club a bit more with you. Your plans for selling it especially."

He stifled the sigh. "Sure. When?"

"How about tonight? You could come round here for dinner. In fact, let's do that. You haven't been for dinner here in years."

It had been a while. These days they met in the club or in restaurants downtown and Kahu had never questioned why Rob had stopped inviting him back to his place. He'd assumed…well, he'd never assumed anything in actual fact. After all, it hadn't mattered to him where they went to discuss business.

Now, though… Was Lily still living with him or did she have her own place somewhere else? Christ, he didn't even know that much.

"I could do," he said noncommittally. "But if you'd rather—"

"I would rather you come to dinner," Rob cut him off with certainty.

"Be nice to have you over. Lily won't mind. You know how she keeps to herself."

How completely fucking wonderful. So Lily did live with her father.

Kahu closed his eyes and toyed briefly with the idea of finding a handy excuse not to go. Which was just insane. What the hell was wrong with him that he was trying to avoid a twenty-year-old? What was he afraid of? She wasn't likely to be doing any naked dancing again with her father around, and he wasn't likely to be pulling her to the ground and ravaging her like an animal.

There was no reason on earth to say no.

"In that case," he said, opening his eyes again, the winter sun shining thin and cold on his face. "I'd love to come."

Lily paused at the top of the stairs, her hand resting on the banister as voices floated up from the hallway down below. Her father's light baritone and then another, deeper voice. A darker, huskier, more sensual sound.

She swallowed, her heartbeat beginning to race.

Kahu.

Her father had mentioned that afternoon when he'd gotten home from work that Kahu Winter would be joining them for dinner. Before she'd gotten sick, he used to like her to be at the dinner table too, but these days he didn't much care what she did. Join them or not, it was up to her.

She didn't want to join them. In fact, she would be quite happy never to see Kahu Winter's handsome face ever again.

The voices faded, going toward the lounge area and Lily let out a soft breath. Then she turned and walked back along the hallway to her bedroom, shutting the door quietly behind her before crossing to the bed and sitting down.

She clenched her fists and then relaxed them a couple of times, a calming technique she'd often used before a performance.

God, she couldn't sit up here all evening in her bedroom, not when she'd spent all afternoon stressing about what was going to happen when he actually arrived. Whether she'd wave casually at him and pretend nothing was wrong, or whether she'd try and get him alone and explain herself. Staying upstairs and avoiding him entirely was very, very attractive.

Coward. You're a fucking coward.

She splayed out her fingers on her knees, her skin pale against the faded blue denim, and all she could think about was the heat of his mouth on her skin, his tongue licking her, his scent around her, his dark eyes on hers. So furious with her.

I don't like being manipulated.

She hadn't intended to. Hadn't even thought that's what she'd been doing. He'd said "seduce me" and so that's what she'd tried to do. And okay, so it had all been about her own pride and her hatred of losing, of failing, but she hadn't wanted to do anything more than get an acknowledgement out of him.

Are you sure? You didn't take your clothes off to get an acknowledgement, cretin. You took your clothes off hoping he'd lose all control and fuck you.

She stared at her hands, the burn of shame prickling through her all of a sudden. Yeah, shit, may as well admit to herself that *was* what she'd been hoping for. She'd also been unable to accept giving up on the whole seduction thing, the competitive, fighting part of her not wanting to admit defeat.

It's all about you and what you want, in other words. Not about what he wants.

Her fingers dug into her knees. Why shouldn't she get what she wanted? Hadn't she fought death for it? Hadn't she put up with enough pain and suffering to earn it?

She gritted her teeth. His concerns about their age difference and the fact that her father was his business partner, seemed ridiculous to her, but clearly they weren't to him. Yet that didn't account for his very real fury at her. Okay, so he said he'd felt manipulated, but why? He could have said no, could have walked away.

And he hadn't. He'd stayed there, watching her. He'd even told her what to do and she'd done it. She'd obeyed him and that had only seemed to make him angrier.

She didn't understand it. She didn't understand what she'd done wrong. Jesus, she'd kill for someone to talk it over with. But there was no one.

A deep and familiar pain shifted in her chest and she couldn't help glancing over at her dressing table, where the single photo she had of her mother stood. A bright summer day and she in the pink tutu her mother had made for her, Judith Andrews standing behind her with her hands on her daughter's shoulders. Same strawberry blonde curls, same pale, finely carved face. Except her mother's eyes had been somewhere between green and blue. Turquoise and beautiful.

What wouldn't she give to have her mother to talk to. But there was no use thinking about shit like that. Her mother was years dead and she'd probably be horrified with her daughter wanting to hook up with a man eighteen years older than she was and an ex-rent boy at that. Not that Lily gave a shit about Kahu's past.

But maybe he does?

Halfway off the bed, she paused at the thought. It was weird to think that a man like Kahu, a man who didn't seem to care what anyone thought of him, might care about the things he'd done in his past.

Yet...why had he been a rent boy in the first place? What had led him to it? And what had happened with Anita Howard, his lover, afterwards?

Unfamiliar curiosity twisted inside her like a skein of tangled wool. For years, her entire focus had been on ballet, a constant and consuming passion. And then, when cancer had come, her focus and passion had shifted, channeled into fighting death and getting better.

A person had never been the subject of that focus before because she'd simply never been interested in anyone enough. But now...

Shit, she'd been going about this seduction business wrong, hadn't she? She'd made it all about herself when actually it was all about the person you wanted to seduce. When it was all about you, that's when it became manipulation. When it was all about them, only then did it become seduction.

Lily straightened, a new certainty filling her. She walked out of her bedroom and went along the hallway to the stairs, her heart thumping. But she didn't hesitate as she went down the stairs, approaching the lounge.

In the beautifully appointed room, the fresh roses in the bowl on the coffee table filling the air with their sweet scent, Kahu was sitting on the couch, leaning forward, his elbows on his knees, hands lightly clasped between them.

He wore faded blue jeans and a midnight blue casual shirt, sleeves rolled up as per usual. A black wool captain's coat was thrown carelessly over the couch cushions beside him.

Her breath caught as memory and reality began to blur in her head.

Of him, sitting on that couch over the years, so tall and big and rangy. An impossibly strong, uncontained and uncontainable presence. A wildness to him that she'd always found so fiercely attractive.

That wildness, that danger, was there still and now she had something else to add to it. The heat of his mouth around her fingers. The glitter of desire in his eyes. That deep, rough voice telling her to touch her clit, to put her fingers in her pussy…

Kahu turned and Lily froze as his dark, intense gaze pinned her to the spot.

"Ah, Lily," her father said. "You remember Mr. Winter, don't you?"

Heat swept through her and she could feel her cheeks flaming. "Uh…y-yeah," she stuttered like a complete fool. "Hi."

The expression on his face gave absolutely nothing away, but the smile he gave her didn't reach his eyes. "Hi, Lily."

Naturally enough, her father didn't notice the tension since he didn't notice anything much about her these days. In fact, it was amazing he'd bothered to introduce her at all. "Anyway," he went on, "as I was saying about the market…"

Kahu turned back to the conversation, as if she'd ceased to exist.

Hurt spread through her, a sharp, uncomfortable feeling, though she wasn't quite sure what she'd expected. He wasn't here for her and it wasn't as if he could talk to her about stuff now anyway, not with her father sitting right in the same room.

You're supposed to be thinking about him and what he wants, not you and your daddy issues.

True, though her daddy issues were another can of worms she didn't want to open up right now.

Ignoring the hurt, Lily cleared her throat. "Uh, sorry, Dad, but what time's dinner?"

A look of irritation crossed his face at the interruption. "Half an hour. Daphne's got something in the oven for us."

"Can I help out? Set the table and stuff?"

Her father waved a hand dismissively. "Whatever you like."

"What about a drink? Would you like—"

"Lily, for God's sake, can't you see I'm talking?" He glared at her. "Just go and do…whatever. Mr. Winter and I have important things to discuss and we don't want to be constantly interrupted."

The words stung. Ever since she'd gotten out of the hospital and come back here to live, it was like anytime she made her father more than vaguely aware of her presence he got irritated. Snapping at her and telling her to go away and do something else. She'd gotten used to it. But somehow, Kahu's presence made it different. Made the words hurt more than they usually did.

She tried to ignore his presence on the couch. "Okay," she muttered. "Suit yourself. If you need anything I'll be in the kitchen."

And she turned away.

Kahu stared at Rob. Behind him he could hear Lily's soft tread fade as she walked away from the doorway and down the hall toward the kitchen.

Dismissed. Like a naughty child.

Had Rob always treated her like that? It disturbed him that he couldn't remember. But then he'd never been this aware of her before. Even when she'd spent the last hour since he'd arrived up in her bedroom, the mere fact she was in the same house weighed on him.

And it was weird. All around him were the reminders of the civilized dinners he'd had with Anita and Rob, and then the business meetings conducted over chess games. And a little girl with big eyes, who'd watched him, fascinated.

Except that little girl wasn't so little anymore. And he'd tasted her.

He could taste her still, her flavor sitting in his mouth, the sweetest reminder of all.

Kahu caught his breath and tried to direct his attention to the present. "Was that really necessary?"

His friend frowned. "Was what necessary?"

Christ, the guy hadn't even realized what he'd said. "Lily. She was only trying to help."

Rob waved a hand. "Oh that. Well, we have important stuff to discuss. I don't know why she's always hanging around the house all the time. I thought she had friends to go see but apparently not."

There was something in the other man's tone Kahu didn't like, though he couldn't put his finger on what it was. "I didn't realize she was still living at home. What is she now? Twenty, right?"

An expression he didn't recognize crossed Rob's face, though he was sure it had something to do with anger. "She's trying to be a dancer, which obviously doesn't pay very well. So she's at home until… Until she manages to make money obviously."

"That's tough," Kahu said carefully. "She doesn't have another job?"

"No." The word was flat.

Interesting. Clearly there was tension between Rob and his daughter.

The sound of orchestral music filled the room and Rob cursed as he fumbled for his phone. "Damn." He glanced down at the screen. "I have to take this, sorry."

"Sure, go ahead."

"Why don't you go help yourself to a beer? You know where they are." Rob got up from the couch and answered the phone, walking over to the windows.

Go get a beer. In the kitchen. Where Lily was.

Perhaps it wasn't a good idea to be alone with her, considering their last interaction. But he couldn't shrug off the way her father had spoken to her. It made him angry, though it didn't make any sense as to why. He just…didn't like it.

Rising from the couch, Kahu went out into the hall and down toward the kitchen at the back of the house.

The décor was farmhouse—not Rob's thing which meant it was probably the work of his long dead wife—and scrupulously clean. Lily stood by the sink, loading things into the dishwasher.

She was in her usual uniform of skinny jeans and converses, a black T-shirt with a long sleeved purple top underneath. Her hair was tied back in a loose ponytail, curls hanging around her fine-boned face.

For once she wasn't wearing her ubiquitous duffel coat and maybe that was a bad thing because he was very conscious of the length of her legs in those jeans and the curve of her breasts beneath her tightly fitting T-shirt. Far more conscious than he wanted to be.

She didn't look at him or stop what she was doing, her movements short and sharp as she tried to jam in a mug in the top drawer, the china clinking. "The beer is in the fridge if that's what you're after."

Kahu ignored that, leaning against the doorframe instead. "Are you okay?"

"I'm fine."

"You're going to break that mug if you're not careful."

She let out a breath and put the mug back on the counter. "Got any other dishwasher-loading suggestions?" Her voice was bright with sarcasm, her features set and tight.

"Your father's a dick," he said quietly. "He had no call to speak to you like that."

Lily lifted a shoulder. "Yeah, well, it's nothing new so don't sweat it."

She was trying to act like it didn't matter. He could spot that a mile off. Which meant, of course, that it did.

"Lily—"

"I don't really want to talk about it." She pushed the dishwasher drawer back in with slightly more force than was strictly necessary and shut the door with a click. Stabbing at a few buttons, she turned it on.

Okay so this more than mattered. She was hurt. What the hell was going on with her and Rob? Why had treated his daughter like a naughty three-year-old? She wasn't a child anymore.

Oh yeah and you have firsthand knowledge of that, don't you?

He took a careful, measured breath. Yes, he knew. She was a woman and he was becoming more and more aware of that with every passing second.

He opened his mouth to say something, but she got in first.

"I'm sorry, Kahu." She turned to face him, her back to the kitchen counter. "I'm sorry about Monday night. I'm sorry about what I did. You should know that it wasn't my intention to manipulate you or anything, I just…" She stopped.

This was *not* what he'd been expecting at all. He crossed his arms, waiting for her to continue.

"I don't like to lose," she eventually went on. "And I don't like to give up. And that little performance in your study was more about me than it was about you." Another hesitation. "Which isn't what seduction is all about."

He really didn't know what to say. He hadn't been anticipating discussing Monday night at all, let alone receiving an apology from her, and it left him feeling like she'd come in and shifted around his favorite room, and nothing was where he thought it was anymore.

She was looking at him now, green eyes shifting into misty gray, the lights above her head highlighting the gold strands in her hair and lashes. And he could see the sincerity in her face—she meant what she'd said all right.

He cleared his throat. "It wasn't entirely your fault. I was the one who agreed to the Monday night sessions in the first place."

"I know, but only because I pushed." She shifted against the counter, her hands behind her, gripping tight as if for balance. "And like I said, that's the problem. It's all about me and what I want. I've never actually asked you what you want."

No one's ever asked you that.

She shifted again, nervously. "So I guess that's what I'm asking you now. What do you want, Kahu?"

The room seemed to spin, the words echoing weirdly in his head. Over the years, after Anita had sent him away, he'd managed to carve out a life that wasn't directed by her. Where he was in charge and he didn't have to give away pieces of himself to other people in return for money or anything else.

Where he made the decisions and did what he wanted, not what other people thought was best for him.

But no one had ever asked him that question. Not any of his lovers, not any of his friends. Not even Eleanor.

His heartbeat had sped up, the sound loud in his ears, almost drowning out the words she'd spoken. What do you want? What do *you* want?

"What do you mean?" His voice sounded thick, unlike himself.

"I mean, what do you want from me? If it's no more Monday night sessions then I can stop. If you don't want to see me again…say the word and you won't."

That's not what you want and you know it.

Yeah, he knew it. Deep in his heart, the knowledge had been there all the time. The decisions he'd been making about Lily were what he thought was best for both of them. Because of their age difference. Because of the business.

But they weren't what he actually *wanted*.

He shifted against the doorframe, because even now he wasn't sure if he should give voice to what he wanted. Saying it aloud made it real. Made it possible. And once she heard it… Jesus. "Are you sure you want to know, sweetheart?"

"I wouldn't have asked if I didn't."

"What I want is not to want you. But it's too late for that."

Her red-gold lashes went wide at the admission, the green in her eyes sparking.

Shit, why was she surprised? She must know he wanted her, especially after Monday.

"Oh…" She swallowed audibly. "If it's too late, then what else?"

It was wrong to say it. Wrong to speak the words aloud. But he'd already broken his no-touching promise. He'd started down this road and now he had no choice but to keep on walking. Besides, as that little interchange with Rob had already made him aware, Lily Andrews wasn't a child anymore.

"I want someone who's mine," he said, his voice not quite level.

"Who's there for me. Who will do exactly what I tell them, when I tell them to do it. I want someone whose sole purpose is to be there for my pleasure. Someone I choose." As he spoke, an inexplicable anger bloomed into life inside him. Because how many times had he had things taken from him? By the clients who'd used him and by the woman who'd rescued him from that life. Oh sure, Anita had given him everything, but only the things she deemed important. She'd never asked whether he was interested in the "culture" she was determined to impart. She'd never asked him whether he'd even wanted to go back to school or university.

She'd just assumed and directed, moving him around like a chess piece on a board. So yeah, fuck, why couldn't he have something he actually wanted for a change? Someone who would give him everything he wanted and demand nothing in return.

Color had crept into her cheeks. "I could be that someone for you," Lily said, her voice quiet but very certain. "I could be yours. You could choose me."

Yes.

His body had already made that decision, or at least his rapidly hardening cock did.

Lily. His. Yes.

Except his brain needed some time to catch up. "I told you I wasn't going to touch you. That was our agreement."

"I realize that. But...you've touched me already, Kahu." She paused, biting her lip. "It could just be for one night and that's it."

Fuck yes!

He fought the instinctive, gut response, because she probably had no idea what she was offering. "Do you really understand what I'm asking for, ballerina?"

"Yes, of course I do."

"No, love. You don't. When I say I want someone who's mine, I mean it. Every decision, every choice, every action would be decided by me, for me." God, the more he said the words, the more he wanted this. Take something for himself. Make it about him.

"Okay. I get that."

"I don't think you do. It means that what you want would be irrelevant. Only what I want is important."

There it was, the uncertainty and fear he'd expected, flickering through her eyes like shadows. "Oh... Would...would you hurt me?"

Something in his chest tightened. Because he knew the answer to that too. "I might. If it gives me pleasure."

Her mouth opened then closed. Another swallow, her gaze dropping away from his to the floor. "I don't want to be hurt."

"No, I don't suppose you do. Pain can be pleasurable as well, but I guess that's not the point. The point is that I want someone to give themselves to me without reservation. Without holding back." Unlike Anita, who'd always withheld a part of herself from him. Even when he'd given her everything he was.

"Don't be silly, Kahu. I don't love you and you don't love me. That's not what this relationship is all about."

But he had loved her, no matter what she'd said.

"Why?" Lily asked. "Why do you need that?"

"Because that's what I want." He wasn't going into the whys, not now and not with her.

"What if I don't want to give you that?"

"Then don't. I can't force anyone into doing this for me. It wouldn't work if force was involved anyway. I want consent, freely given, for anything I might want to do." He wasn't into non-con fantasies, though he knew people who were. No, the image that made his mouth go dry was someone giving themselves to him. And not because he asked, but because they wanted to do something for him. Because they wanted to be his.

Someone?

Okay. Lily. Her.

She was looking at him warily and he didn't like it. "But…what if I say yes and then when we get halfway through the night you start doing stuff that hurts. That I don't want. You're saying that's not important?"

He shook his head. "No, I'm not saying that. I'm saying that *I'm* important. What I want. And if what I want is to see you come, to hear your pleasure, then I'm not going to push you hard into doing something that doesn't give you any."

She was blushing again. "Okay, okay. I just…don't know anything about this stuff."

"I know you don't. And that's why you'd better be careful with what you're offering me, ballerina. It's a gift I want. And a sacrifice. But you have to be fully aware of that going in."

She was silent a long minute. "Have you ever done this before with anyone? Has anyone…uh…given themselves to you before?"

"No."

"Why not?"

"Because no one's ever asked." And he spoke the truth because she deserved to have it. "No one except you."

That got to her, he could see it in the brief flare of green in her eyes. But then she looked away again, the toe of one shoe scuffing at the kitchen lino. "We can't do this any other way? Does it have to be so absolute?"

He paused, thinking about it. About what he wanted from her and how it was possible for there to be another way. But another way wasn't what he wanted. He didn't quite know why it had to be her in particular either. Perhaps it was because she was the one who'd roused him after a long period of feeling nothing. Or perhaps it was only because she kept challenging him. There was, of course, the titillation factor too—everything about being with her would be wrong and that kind of "wrongness" had always attracted him.

In the end, though, only one thing was important and that was he wanted what he wanted. End of story.

"No," he said, "there is no other way. It's this or nothing."

"Why?"

"Because if I'm going to go to hell for screwing you, ballerina, then I may as well make it count."

She let out a breath, staring down at the floor. "It's a big ask, Kahu."

"That's why I'm not asking you. You wanted to know what I want, so I told you."

Lily shifted again. Her fingers were white where they clutched the edge of the counter. "And if I don't want to do this?"

Disappointment snagged him, but he refused to acknowledge it. "Then you don't. But our Monday nights will have to stop."

"That's hardly fair."

He shrugged. "It's the way it is." No way he was going to put up with sitting in a room with a hard-on, knowing he wouldn't be able to touch her. He wasn't that much of a masochist.

"Hey," Rob called from down the other end of the hall. "Can you grab me a beer too?"

"Sure," he called back. Pushing himself away from the doorframe, he went over to the fridge and got out two beer bottles. The bottle opener was in the drawer where she was standing and it wasn't a good thing to get near her, not here, but he'd never been very good at being good.

Letting the fridge door fall closed, he slowly walked over to where she stood and she watched him come closer, her eyes wide. He stopped, inches away from her, smelling the light, musky, feminine scent of her, flowers and something else. It made him hard, made him remember the taste of her, salty and tart.

She blinked at him, her gaze falling to his mouth and back to meet his eyes again.

Tension pulled tight.

"I need the bottle opener," he said, breaking it.

She flushed. "Oh…uh…sure." Turning, she pulled open the drawer and handed it to him.

Yeah, he was a dick for getting into her space, especially when he was going to have to go back out to see Rob with a slowly hardening cock. But he hadn't been able to resist. This might be the last time he'd ever get close.

He took the opener and opened the bottles then gave it back to her. "I won't expect you Monday, Lily."

She put it back in the drawer. "I haven't said no yet."

"Like I said, I won't expect you." He turned and began to walk out of the kitchen.

"And what will you do if I turn up?"

He didn't stop. "I'll send you away."

But he knew, deep down, he wouldn't.

Chapter Nine

Lily paid the driver then got out the taxi, pulling her coat more tightly around her as she stepped out onto the sidewalk. It was still shitty and cold, but at least the rain had stopped, which was a bonus.

She turned and looked at the building the taxi had dropped her off outside of, black iron railings and ivy-covered walls. Old and distinguished. Except of course there was nothing distinguished about what went on inside those ivy-covered walls.

Jesus. What was she doing here? Was she really going to do this?

But no. Thinking was what she'd been doing all weekend and she was sick of it. She'd made her decision. She wasn't going to go into second-guessing herself all over again.

She walked up the steps to the blue front door of the Auckland Club and knocked. Loudly.

He'd said he'd send her away. Time to put that to the test.

Her heartbeat had sped up and her mouth was dry and she was probably insane for wanting to do this, but nevertheless, here she was. She didn't even know what had been the thing that had made her decide to do it. Whether it was the fact that he'd told her he wouldn't see her again if she didn't, or that no one had ever asked him what he wanted. She almost couldn't believe that. His reputation as a womanizer was entrenched and it seemed inconceivable that there hadn't been at least one woman who'd asked him that question. Apparently not.

There had been attraction in the thought of being that woman. Of being the only one who'd ever asked. Of being the only one he'd ever wanted it from. Yet that was only a part of the reason she'd decided to come here. There was probably a little bit of her fighting spirit in there as well, the stubborn part of her that wouldn't admit defeat.

Largely though, she was here because he wanted something from her. And she wanted to give it to him. She was curious and every time she thought about him, she ached. She couldn't stop thinking about it.

The cold wind swirled around her, making her shiver, though it probably wasn't only the wind's fault.

She was scared, yes, but she was here now and she wasn't going to leave. It would only be one night and she knew that if she didn't do it, she'd probably regret it for the rest of her life.

The door opened suddenly but it wasn't Kahu. It was the club's bouncer, Mike.

Shit.

"Uh...hi Mike," she said. "Can I come in? I think Mr. Winter is expecting me."

The guy said nothing, just stood aside and gestured to her to come in.

Holy shit. Did that mean...?

Realizing she was standing there staring like a lunatic, she stepped into the club's foyer, her heart racing.

"Mr. Winter is in the study," Mike said, closing the door behind her. "Go in when you're ready."

She nodded. Okay, so he wasn't going to send her away like he'd said.

Slowly, she walked down the hallway, her heartbeat now thundering like a plane taking off, before pausing outside the familiar study door.

Seriously, she had to get a grip on herself. He might even have changed his mind and wanted to see her to give her another lecture. Tell her in no uncertain terms that nothing would happen between them. Or something.

That would be a pity, though, especially considering she'd spent at least an hour on her appearance beforehand. She wasn't used to dressing up for someone but she'd wanted to make the effort for him. Show him she meant what she said. She'd indulged in a scented bath and smoothed on her favorite body lotion before spending a good twenty minutes figuring out what to wear. Eventually she'd settled on her black lace dress with a silver shift on underneath. A subtle but classy—she hoped—combination. She didn't wear heels but she didn't think her black Docs looked too stupid with the dress.

Anyway, if all that wasn't to his taste then she'd brought along something that might be: her pointe shoes.

Bracing herself, Lily opened the door and stepped into the room.

It was warm, the fire obviously having been lit for some time, the warm glow of it lighting up the dim space. And Kahu standing in front of it, watching her.

Everything seemed to draw tight, that thick, dense energy filling the space between them again.

He was dressed all in black, his presence tall and dark. Powerful. His inky gaze was enigmatic and for a second he seemed like a complete stranger to her, nothing to do with the young man who'd winked at her over the table once when she'd been a kid, or the cynical, disreputable rake who'd played chess and shocked her with his dirty mouth.

Her hands shook so she stuffed them into the pockets of her coat as she shut the door. "You told me you'd send me away if I turned up."

"Yeah, well, I lied."

There was a silence, the only sound the fire crackling in the hearth.

"Still," Lily said, struggling with nervousness and fear. "Looks like you were expecting me."

"Mike saw you get out of the taxi."

"Oh."

"And I had the fire going in here anyway." The fire leapt behind him, the light glossing over his black hair. "Why are you here, Lily? Why did you decide to come?"

She walked forward until she stood behind his usual chair then put her hands on the back of it, wanting something to hold onto to so she didn't fidget like a kid. "A few reasons. I'm curious and I want you. And if this is the only way I can have you, then I'll take it." She met his gaze. "And because no one's ever given you this before."

"It scares you, though."

There was no point in denying it, even though she hated the acknowledgment. "I guess. A little. The unknown is always scary, isn't it?"

"Is it me? Do I scare you?"

She blinked, not having thought about it before. "You're a bit scary, yeah," she said slowly, trying to pinpoint what it was that she felt. "But not because I'm afraid you're a serial killer or anything. More because of…" She trailed off, her breath catching as she realized suddenly where all this nervousness was coming from.

She *was* afraid of him. Not because he was physically stronger than she was or that he would hurt her. No, it was far more complex than that. It was because of what he could make her feel. What he'd already made her feel. Out of control. Helpless…

Those emotions that had haunted her at her sickest. Those emotions that had followed her home once she was better and stuck around in the shape of her father and his distancing techniques.

She hated those feelings.

"Because of what?" Kahu asked. "If you're going to do this, Lily, I need to know the truth."

Her fingers dug into the material on the back of the chair. "I don't like not being in control," she acknowledged. "And I'm afraid you'll make me give that up."

"And I will, I told you that."

"Well, that's why I'm afraid of you."

There was a pause, the tension still crackling between them.

Eventually he said, "The die isn't cast yet. I'm not holding you to anything while we're in this room."

The nervous tension in her chest loosened a notch and she let out a breath she hadn't realized she'd been holding. "Oh. Okay then."

"I've got some things I need to say in any case." Kahu moved over to the drinks cabinet and got out their usual tumblers, pouring out some scotch. "Why don't you sit down?"

Lily did so, dumping her satchel on the floor beside the chair. He came over to her and held out the tumbler. She took it with a muttered thanks, gulping down a mouthful to soothe the nervousness still pulsing through her.

He went back to his own chair, sitting down and leaning forward, his glass held loosely between his hands, elbows on his knees. There was something very controlled about his posture. As if he was restraining himself somehow.

Was that for her sake? She shifted in her chair, not sure what to think about that. "So what did you want to say?"

He was silent a moment longer, then he said, "I'm not a challenge for you to overcome or a way to prove yourself, understand?"

The intensity in his night-dark eyes was unmistakable and she felt a shiver go through her. She nodded, her voice too thick to speak.

"And I know what I'm asking for is major, believe me, I know. I've been the one doing the giving before and it's not easy." He paused, took a sip of his drink. "It's a matter of trust, Lily. So if you don't trust me, you may as well walk out that door right now."

"I do trust you."

"Enough to give yourself totally to me? Enough to give me the control? Enough to let me make all the decisions about what's right for you and your body?"

Okay, so maybe that needed thinking over a little more. She raised her glass and took another healthy swallow too. "Tell me why you need it, Kahu," she asked as she put the glass down on the table again. "I think you owe me that."

He didn't answer immediately, his gaze on hers, the look on his face unreadable. "I don't owe you anything, ballerina." His tone was mild but she heard the steel running through it.

And suddenly she knew that unless he told her, this wasn't going to happen. If she was going to give him everything, trust him, then she wanted this at least from him in return.

"You want me to trust you," she said. "Then I want to know why I should."

"The whys don't matter. All that matters is that you do."

"They might not matter to you but they do to me."

His features hardened. "What you want doesn't matter, I told you that."

Bizarrely, she felt her eyes prickle. Like she was going to cry or some stupid shit. Which was weird because this shouldn't matter so much. She should be able to get up and walk away from him if he wasn't going to give her this one thing. It should be easy. It shouldn't feel as if she was losing something she'd wanted desperately.

"Then I can't do this," she said thickly.

Another of those impossible, heavy silences fell. And the look on his face made that ridiculous prickle behind her eyes worse because it was so angry.

"If I'm going to give you everything," she whispered, "is it so wrong to want a little something from you in return?"

He looked away, down at the glass in his hands, silent for so long she thought he wasn't going to answer. Then he said, his voice so quiet she barely heard him, "I gave everything I was to Anita, but she never gave herself to me in return. She always held something back. Oh, she gave me lots of things, lots of opportunities. But never what I actually wanted." He raised his head, met her gaze. "So that's what I want now. I want to feel what it's like to have someone give themselves to me wholly and without reservation. Just once."

Her chest felt tight, her throat thick with emotion. Because she saw pain in his eyes. Pain and anger. He'd loved Anita and for some reason the woman hadn't loved him in return, which seemed wrong. Unfair. Because Kahu Winter was a good man. A strong, intelligent, passionate man. If a man like that loved you, why wouldn't you love him in return? How could you *not* fall in love with him?

Something shifted inside her heart. Something she didn't want to acknowledge. A possibility…

You could love him.

No, love was not on the agenda. Love had never been on the agenda. She was only twenty for Christ's sake. She had stuff to do, like that audition, a career in ballet.

Like losing her virginity.

Lily reached out and grabbed her glass, drained it then set it back down with a click. "In that case, I want to do this. I want to do this for you."

Kahu stared at her for a long moment. "Be sure, Lily. Because once we leave this room, once we go upstairs, I'm not going to let you have this choice again."

She didn't know why that quiet assurance made the breath catch hard in her throat, why it chased little chills over her skin. But one thing she did know. "I'm sure."

Something dark flared in his eyes. "You need a word. Something that'll tell me I've pushed too far that isn't no."

Oh Jesus, what was she getting herself into? "Why can't it be no? Shouldn't that be enough?"

"It isn't. I will push, Lily, make no mistake. Because you might think you'll be fine about giving me everything now, but when the time comes you may change your mind. It'll be exposing and you'll be afraid. Venturing out of your comfort zone is always scary." He didn't move, his expression intent. "But I'll push you out of it and you won't like it. You might say no and I'll keep going, and you'll have to trust that I know what I'm doing." His voice dropped, becoming rough. "Sometimes the greatest pleasure can be found on the other side of fear. Sometimes surrendering control can be the best thing there is."

The chills increased, goose bumps rising over her skin, her breathing coming faster. Those words should have terrified her and yet they didn't. They were seductive, a siren call to something deep inside of her, a part of herself that yearned for safety, for someone to hold her, care for her. Tell her not to worry. To take away the burden of all that control.

Fuck, she was trembling and she didn't even know why. She clasped her hands together to stop the shake. "That sounds like experience talking."

He swirled the scotch in his glass but didn't drink, watching her. "I've done it, yes. For Anita. For the clients I had before that, though that really wasn't about pleasure. But now I want to try the other side. I want to hold the reins." His hand stilled. "It's a gift, Lily. And I know the value of it. I would never treat it as nothing."

She could hear the sincerity in his voice and it helped calm her. "I know you wouldn't." And she meant it. "So, I have to think of a word?"

"Yes. The more out of context the better."

"Um... What about 'ballet'? It's something I'll remember anyway." And then, feeling suddenly self-conscious, "Or is that too stupid?"

A faint smile curved his mouth and the nervousness in her chest loosened another notch. "No, it's not too stupid. Ballet is perfect."

"Oh good." She eyed him since he was looking at her as if waiting for something. "What?"

The smile lingered on his mouth. "Did you bring your ballet shoes?"

And just like that, the nervousness was back, bringing with it the chills and the shivers, the flutter of desire deep inside her. "Yes," she whispered. "I did."

He nodded once, lifting his glass and drinking the rest of the liquid in it before putting it back down on the table beside him. "Then let's go."

Kahu got her to follow him as they went upstairs, to his own apartment that was situated above the club.

The door was down the end of a short hallway and he opened it up for her, standing aside so she could enter first, stepping into a large room with high, ornate ceilings and large windows that had views out onto Auckland's large, green inner city park. Ivy partly covered the windows, making the light dim and green, like being underwater.

The floor was of dark, polished wood, the walls plain white. There was a low couch under the windows, the leather cracked and old, a velvet blanket half covering it. A couple of eastern style rugs in blues and reds gave the room color, while lots of bookcases stuffed with books and knickknacks gave it character.

It was warm, though there was no fireplace up here, which meant he must have some kind of central heating going on in the room.

She swallowed, clutching her coat around her, feeling awkward and restless and jumpy as Kahu shut the door, the sound of the club downstairs cutting off completely.

"That's some sound-proofing you've got there," she said inanely.

He turned from the door and came toward her. And Lily felt herself tense up, her mouth dry as the desert at midday, her lungs fighting for the oxygen that Kahu had apparently shut out when he'd closed the door.

Yet he stopped in front of her without touching, his hands loose at his sides. He seemed more relaxed than he'd been downstairs and that might have made her feel less tense if not for that black glitter in the depths of his eyes. The one that told her he was hungry. For her.

"Don't speak." His voice was quiet, yet she could hear the command in the words. "I only want to hear you if you need to use that word we talked about."

Instinctive protests filled her mouth, but she bit them back. Hell, if he wanted her to be quiet, then she had no problem with it. She didn't know what to say anyway.

Nodding, she kept her lips shut tight.

He looked down at her, not speaking, the brutally handsome lines of his face unyielding. And she felt the shakes return, her heartbeat going into overdrive. He was so close, that spicy scent of his, the one that reminded her of summer, making her want to bury her face in the warm cotton of his shirt, cover herself with heat.

"Don't move," he murmured, as if he could sense the restlessness and nervous tension inside her and knew what she was desperate to do.

So she stood her ground, not knowing where to put her hands so keeping them tightly clutching onto her coat.

Then he cupped her face between his palms.

Any air that had been in her lungs rushed out of it as the heat of his skin met hers. And she trembled all over. She couldn't look away from the inky blackness of his eyes, the darkness seeming to pull her in, suck her under.

"Breathe, Lily," he whispered.

She inhaled, sucking down a breath like he'd told her.

And then his mouth covered hers.

Shock. Heat. A bolt of lightning straight through her heart.

She couldn't stop shaking. When had she been kissed last? She couldn't remember. But soon even that thought had vanished along with everything else in the entire world. The only thing that existed was now, this moment, Kahu's mouth on hers.

Achingly gentle, his thumbs easing down her lower lip so he could slide his tongue into her mouth, beginning to explore her slowly, tasting her as he did so.

A sound she hadn't intended to make escaped her, a low moan, and she shut her eyes, dizzy as the blood rushed to her head. Or maybe that was the scotch she'd drunk, the scotch she could taste on him, smoky and hot. She found herself leaning in to him, her mouth opening farther, wanting more.

"Keep still," he murmured, his lips brushing hers.

Dammit, no. But she did as she was told because she'd promised, struggling to stay still while his thumbs stroked lightly over her cheekbones then down along her jaw, his fingers trailing across the sensitive column of her neck and throat. Fire sparked, heat on frozen ground, waking parts of her she hadn't realized were there.

She knew how sensitive skin could be, when needles penetrated and scalpels cut. When pain became so pervasive that even the brush of the hospital gown made her want to cry in agony. But she'd never known it could be sensitive to pleasure as well. So that all she wanted was to be touched, stroked, to have his hands on her. Where it didn't matter what part of her body he touched as long as he was touching it.

And the kiss went on and on, the moment lasting forever as he tipped her head back farther, exploring deeper, becoming hotter, until her whole soul was drawn thin with want. To press against him. To put her hands on his chest. Touch him the way he was touching her.

Yet way before she was ready, he released her, leaving her shaking like a leaf as she looked up into his face.

Had he felt that? Had he been shattered by that kiss too?

The bronzed skin of his cheekbones was flushed and his jaw was tight, his eyes glittering. So yeah, maybe. She hoped so because she didn't want to be alone in this.

And perhaps he heard her unspoken thought because he said, in a voice that wasn't quite steady, "You taste like heaven, ballerina. But I think other parts of you might taste even better and I can't wait." He took a step back, giving her some space. "Take your clothes off. And then I want you to put your pointe shoes on."

Somehow the nervousness and tension she'd felt earlier had gone. Like the kiss had taken it from her. So that she was able to turn away from him and go over to the couch without trembling. Able to deal with the buttons of her coat and slide it off, leaving her in her lace dress.

"Wait," he said softly and she did, standing with her back to him, her breathing getting shorter and shorter. "That dress is beautiful, but I think it would look better if you had nothing on underneath it."

Oh, she could do that. Indeed she could.

Her hands were shaking again but she managed to get the overdress off over her head and the silver shift underneath it. Then she took her bra off and slid her panties down her legs, stepping out of them before grabbing the lace dress and putting it on again. The feeling of the lace against her hardened nipples drew shudders from her and as she sat on the couch to take her boots off, she had to clench her thighs, the sensation heightened by the coolness of the leather against her bare butt.

It made it even worse to know he was watching her every move, his gaze on her face, seeing everything that passed over it.

She tried to concentrate on getting her boots off and once those were done, taking the pointe shoes out of her satchel. It was as she lifted her foot into the shoe that he stepped forward, kneeling at her feet in a fluid, controlled movement, his hands coming to rest on hers, stilling them.

"I'll do that." And he did, holding her foot and sliding the pointe shoe onto it.

She couldn't stop the outrush of breath that escaped her as his fingers brushed her sensitive instep, the shock of the touch working its way up her calf. And unease twisted inside her.

This was too much. She couldn't cope with this, she just couldn't.

Yet she stayed still as he wound the ribbons tight around her ankle, not quite how she would do them, but good enough for their purposes. Then he moved on to her other foot. "You're bruised," he murmured, looking down at her toes.

She flushed, self-conscious again. Ballet dancer feet. Not pretty. Did he want her to answer? Explain?

Like he knew every thought that went through her head, he glanced at her. "You can speak."

"Pointe shoes hurt sometimes." Jesus, was that thick, husky voice really hers? "It's no big deal, though. All part of being a dancer."

He nodded then glanced down at the foot in his hand. "You won't have to wear them long tonight." Picking up the shoe, he slid it on then began tying the ribbon, taking a ridiculously long time about it too, so that her breathing got faster and her skin prickled. So that she had to clench her thighs tighter because she didn't know what he planned and the not knowing was making her ache. Making her breath clog in her throat.

Eventually he finished and let go of her foot. But he didn't move, his hungry gaze moving down from her face to take in her breasts, partly visible through the lace, before moving down even farther over her hips and stomach, to focus steadfastly between her thighs.

Her heart kicked hard in her chest.

His hands settled on her knees and her heart kicked even harder as he pushed them apart. "Lie back," he murmured.

Every muscle in her body tightened. Fear crept up on her, fear of losing it in front of him. Losing her grip on her body. On herself. Because he would make her, she already knew that. If she was trembling so hard she couldn't stop now, how bad would it get when he really started touching her?

Kahu's gaze caught hers. His palms were warm on her knees, his thumbs making her shiver as he gently stroked the insides of them. "Do you want to say the word, Lily?"

"Yes," she croaked, hating herself for admitting it.

"Fear won't hurt you. But if you feel you have to say it then say it."

She opened her mouth but this time nothing came out.

He stared at her a long moment, his thumbs stroking lazily. "You know what I think?" he said softly. "I think you don't want this to end. I think you don't want to give into this fear. Because I can see how turned on you are. I can smell it too. But understand that you're not the only one, okay? I'm so hard for you I think I'd break if you walked out on me now."

Were those tears in her eyes? Was that what was making her vision blur?

"You're a dancer, Lily" he went on. "Tell me what the music means to you."

She blinked hard to clear her vision, her throat thick, not sure where he was going with this. "It…leads me, I guess. It lets me know how to move and when. It shows me the way."

"Right. So I need you to think of me as your music." His thumbs stopped moving, sharp points of heat against her skin. "And you need to trust me to lead you, to show you the way. Does that make sense?"

The words found an echo inside her, a response, and she stared stupidly at him for a second as the meaning penetrated.

The music was part of the dance. Without it there were only forms. Only position. Without it she couldn't move, couldn't find her way through. But when she had it, she gripped on tight to it. Let it move her, lead her. And she trusted it to hold her when she leapt and catch her when she came back down again.

The music was her guide. It set her free.

I am your music. Trust me.

Oh, she could do that. She was a dancer and music was the air she breathed.

Lily took a breath "Okay." And one by one, she relaxed her muscles, slowly lying back against the couch.

This time when he pushed her knees apart she let him, shuddering as he slid her dress up, his gaze lowered between her thighs to where she was bare and wet and aching. His fingers trailed up and down the sensitive skin of her inner thighs, making her want to twist and turn in his grip, ease the restless feeling inside her.

"Christ, you're beautiful." His voice was rougher now, a sensual rasp against her skin. "Look at you, all wet and hot for me. But I'm not going to go easy on you, sweetheart. You made me so hard last time, with your fingers in your pussy." His thumbs trailed up the insides of her thighs and she began to pant. "I know you want to move, want to come, but I'm not going to let you. Not yet." He leaned in, his breath warm and she had to bite her lip, trembling as the pulse of desire began to beat hard inside her.

"You know what I did after I left you last Monday?" he whispered. "I had to go upstairs and jerk off before I could do anything. That pissed me off. All week I had to go around with the taste of you in my mouth.

So I'm going to punish you for that, ballerina. I'm going to eat that pretty little cunt of yours until you're screaming."

The hard, brutal sound of the word sent a kind of shock through her. And then his hands were pressing hard on her thighs, holding them wide, and she was panting, trembling with the anticipation of the moment.

He lowered his head, his breath hot on her skin, his thumbs parting her tender flesh, the sensation making her moan. And then his tongue licked a hot path straight up the center of her sex.

Her hips jerked against his hands, a cry escaping her. The sensation was sharp, a vicious twist of pleasure made even more intense by the anticipation. And when he did it again, she let out another cry, the sound echoing in the silent room.

She wanted to close her legs, protect herself against the onslaught but his hold was unbreakable. He bent over her like a panther over a kill, licking in long, slow strokes that caught her in the sharp grip of ecstasy.

Lily shut her eyes, trying to lessen the sensations but he wasn't having any of that.

"Open your eyes," he ordered in a rough, low voice and she found herself obeying.

He crouched at her feet, long, blunt fingers dark against the pale skin of her thighs, a feral, hungry look in his gaze. "Watch me, ballerina. I want you to watch what I do to you."

So she did, biting her lip hard as he lowered his head again, as his tongue found her clit and began to move in light, teasing circles. Then she felt his fingers trail lower, to the entrance of her body, stroking before he slid one inside her.

Again, her hips jerked at the unfamiliar sensation, heat prickling all over her body. She groaned as his finger began to move in a slow rhythm, a second joining the first, stretching her gently. His tongue licked over her clit in the same kind of maddening rhythm and she couldn't keep still, trying to ease the intensity building inside her.

It was getting too much and she couldn't control it. And that terrified her. Like she was being pushed inexorably over a cliff she couldn't see the bottom of, with nothing to hold onto, to grab to stop herself from falling.

"Kahu," she groaned. "Please...I can't...stop..."

His movements became slow and focused. "Remember what I am, ballerina." His breath feathered over her thighs, adding to the sensations. "Remember to trust me."

Yes. He was the music, wasn't he? Which meant she had to.

Lily flung an arm over her hot face as his tongue slicked over her again, as she felt his fingers twist then curl inside her, the friction increasing, until the pleasure burst through her in an overwhelming flood, pushing her off that cliff...falling and falling, tearing a scream from her as she fell.

Afterwards she lay there against the couch, her arm heavy over her face. She felt hot and sweaty, like moving was an impossibility. The warmth of Kahu's body between her legs shifted and she blinked as he pulled her arm away from her face.

His gaze was hungry. "On your feet."

Stand? After that? He had to be kidding.

"I don't think—" she began, her voice croaky.

But he was reaching for her, lifting her up from the couch and setting her on her feet, his hands on her hips to steady her. Dazed, she looked up at him, the breath catching in her throat as he fisted his hand in her hair, pulling her head back. He didn't give her a moment to speak or get her bearings, his mouth coming down on hers in another soul-stealing kiss. Except this time it wasn't gentle like the last one had been. This one was hard and hungry, demanding a response.

She could taste herself on his mouth and instinctively she wanted to pull back, but his hand was in her hair, keeping her right where he wanted her. And God, the kiss was so hot. So intense. It turned her inside out.

He devoured her like she was his favorite dessert, holding her still, his other hand in the small of her back. And she was surrounded, his tall, powerful body at her front, his arms curved around her.

Her hands rested against his chest and she could feel the hard muscle beneath the cotton of his shirt. Iron strength and heat, so much heat. And passion. And fury. It was like being in the middle of a hurricane, surrounded by a storm, overwhelmed by it, unable to resist the sheer power of it.

You can't handle this. He's too much for you.

A thread of fear wound through the back of her consciousness, though it was too late to stop now. She had that word she could say and she had no doubt he'd stop if she wanted him to. But saying it would mean giving up and there was no way she was doing that.

Of course there is a third way. Surrender.

Stupid. She was doing that already, wasn't she? Wasn't not saying that word surrendering?

Kahu released her, leaving her breathing wildly, her heartbeat out of control. The aftershocks of the orgasm he'd given her were bright bursts of electricity in her bloodstream, making her feel slow and heavy, dizzy.

His hands settled on her hips again, turning her around, unresisting, so she faced the couch with him at her back. "Legs apart and on your toes, ballerina." His mouth was near her ear, his breath warm against her skin. "Show me your form."

Her body was obeying before her brain had time to catch up, shifting into first position then her heels lifting, rising up on the toes of her pointe shoes. "Good girl," he murmured approvingly. "Now put your hands on the back of the couch and bend over."

Again she was moving before she could think about it, reaching out to balance herself against the back of the couch and bending, feeling her dress lift against the backs of her thighs as she did so. Leaving her open and exposed.

Her pulse thumped in her head, her thighs trembling. What the hell did he want with her in this position? With her legs apart and butt out?

You know...

She sucked in a breath, trying and failing to calm down.

"Stay like that," he said.

And then she heard him move away, his footsteps fading.

Her mind was racing, her mouth dry. She felt so hot and yet at the same time she was shivering. What was happening to her? What the fuck was he doing to her?

Yet she didn't move, holding the position, the tremble in her thighs becoming more acute, which was just ridiculous because she'd held worse positions and for longer.

Some time passed, she didn't know how long. And then...hands, sliding up her thighs, easing her dress up to her hips. She choked out a gasp, not expecting the touch since she hadn't heard him return.

"Easy, sweetheart," Kahu whispered, one hand slipping between her thighs. "It's only me." His fingers pushed gently inside her, stretching her, drawing another moan from her. "So wet and tight. I like it. You're all ready, ballerina." The sound of a zipper being drawn down, the crinkle of foil. "I'm going to fuck you now so you'd better hang on tight. Because virginity or not, I'm not holding back."

She was shaking again, every part of her. Aching for him and yet afraid. A fear she couldn't have articulated even if she'd wanted to. Like this was a step she could never come back from if she took it.

Ballet…that's the word. Ballet.

Kahu's fingers between her legs, opening her. The hard press of his cock against her, delicate tissues stretching around him as he pushed into her. Relentless. Inexorable. Her body giving way before his, surrounding him.

She panted, struggling to breathe. It didn't hurt but it was uncomfortable and there was pressure and she couldn't work out whether the feeling was good or not.

Ballet. You can say it.

No, she didn't want to say it. She could do this. She could handle it.

His hand slid around to her stomach, fingers spreading out over her abdomen. Holding her there. Then he pulled back and thrust. Hard.

Oh fuck. She gasped at the sensation, but he didn't give her any time to get used to it, thrusting again, even harder.

Jesus, the feeling was…intense. A primal, raw thing that she couldn't escape from, with his hand holding her in place as he continued to move hard and deep, making her take everything he gave her.

"Kahu…" His name was barely a cracked whisper and she didn't even know why she'd said it.

His hand pressed harder, while the other slid up her torso to cup one breast, his thumb rubbing roughly over her nipple, the lace adding another layer of sensation to the already sensitive tip.

A strange sob sat in her throat. Because this was too much and she couldn't deal with it. Instinct had her wanting to fight against the overwhelming pleasure, to hold out, not let her body be defeated by it. But the way it was building…so raw, fierce. She wasn't going to be able to stop it. She was going to be swept away. Helpless.

"Kahu…please… Oh…God…I can't…"

"You're fighting me." His voice, rough and low against her skin. "You're hanging on. So don't, understand? Let go." His fingers on her stomach moved lower, the tip of his index finger pressing against her clit. "Give yourself to me."

The pleasure grew teeth, becoming agonizing, digging into her skin. But how could she do that when letting go felt like losing? Like dying?

Tears started in her eyes, the sob choking her. She'd fought for so long she couldn't give up just like that. "I can't… Kahu, I can't."

"You promised me, Lily." He was so hot against the bare skin of her butt, his hands on her hard and sure. Leaving her with nowhere to escape to. Nowhere to run. "And I'm going to hold you to that promise."

Lily shut her eyes, her knuckles white against the back of the couch, her body drawn tight as a bow, muscles screaming. "I'm sorry," she whispered brokenly. "I…can't…"

His finger slid against her clit, his cock pushing deeper, shoving her forward, making her muscles have to flex to keep her balance. "I'm the music, ballerina." Again he stroked his finger, sending white-hot pleasure rolling through her. Making her shudder. Making her burn. "Dance with me."

Dance? How could she dance when her body was being overwhelmed? *Because you're fighting it.*

She gasped aloud, the breath leaving her lungs in a rush. Yes, he was right. She was fighting it. And not just now, she'd been fighting it ever since she'd recovered. Fighting the music. Fighting her body. Fighting her passion.

That's why it was so hard. That's why she'd failed her audition.

Because you don't fight the music. You surrender to it.

Tears seeped from beneath her closed lids, her breath coming in short, ragged gasps. And she loosened her grip then let go.

Pleasure burned through her, a fire overwhelming her every defense.

The sob in her throat became a moan, a cry, the hand on her stomach feeling like he was lifting her, launching her into the sky. The push of his cock inside her forcing her higher.

The ecstasy of it broke her.

"Kahu," she whispered, ragged and raw. "Oh…Kahu…"

The climax crashed through her like a storm through a fragile glass window, shattering her, breaking her into a thousand tiny pieces.

Never to be repaired.

Chapter Ten

He felt her pussy clench tight around him, sobs racking her, and she was so hot and tight and wet it was all he could do not to lose himself in the pleasure that had a chokehold on him.

But he resisted. For the first time in years, he was in absolute fucking control and he wasn't ready to give that up for the mindless pleasure of orgasm quite yet.

There was no rush anyway. She was his for the entire night. She'd given him the gift of both her virginity and her surrender, and he wanted to savor both as long as he could.

Slowly he stroked a hand down her graceful back, relishing the sheen of sweat under that sexy black lace dress and the hot clasp of her body around his still-hard cock.

She was panting, her head hanging down between her trembling arms, her hands clutching white-knuckled on the back of the couch.

He'd been inside many women but he couldn't think of another time he'd felt like this, a strange combination of emotional satisfaction without the release.

Christ, she'd fought him. Fought the pleasure he was giving her. And he didn't know why that was, but he'd managed to get her to let go, to surrender herself to it and to him. And feeling her body push back against him and hearing her sob out her climax like that had been worth everything. Made him feel like a fucking god.

Yeah, he might go to hell for screwing his business partner's virgin daughter but, shit, he was going to go happy.

He let his palm curve over her butt, her skin smooth and silky beneath his hand. He'd said what she wanted didn't matter, but of course it did. And being the giver of pleasure was such a rush.

Sometimes in bed with Anita, she'd let him take a dominant role but never for long enough or often enough. She'd always told him she preferred to call the shots and because he'd loved her, he'd let her.

But even in bed, doing what she told him, he'd had the sense that she was holding back from him and it had been so frustrating, driving him crazy. Like a reward she held constantly out of reach, a piece of her soul she kept hidden. It wouldn't have been so bad if he hadn't given her everything he was, if he hadn't broken himself wide open for her. But he had.

Lily is not Anita.

No, she wasn't and maybe working out his own deal on her wasn't fair. But that was too bad. This feeling of control, of power, was too good and he wanted more. He was going to push and push. Get every little piece of her. She would be his completely before this night was over and she would give herself willingly.

And he would be the one holding the reins for a fucking change.

Gently he eased himself out of her, gratified by her soft moan as he did so. She swayed, her knees buckling, so he tightened his arm around her, holding her so she didn't fall. "Let go of the couch, Lily," he murmured, taking the slight weight of her as she did so, her body shaking as she tried to stand upright.

Hell. She was still on her damn toes.

Remembering the bruises on her feet and the blood blister under one of her nails, he lifted her into his arms, cradling her like a child.

She kept her eyes closed, her skin deeply flushed. Red-gold curls stuck to her damp forehead and there were tears on her cheeks.

His heart caught, like a fishhook snagging on a rock. It had been intense and he'd pushed her hard for her first time. Too hard maybe.

He turned, carrying her across the lounge and through a set of double doors that led to the short hallway and his bedroom. The room was dark, the curtains pulled.

Kahu carried her across to the bed under the windows and laid her down onto it. Then he finally got rid of the condom in the wastebasket near the chest of drawers. His cock ached, wanting to be sheathed in her flesh. But he could wait. There was plenty of time for that.

He began to undress, leaving his clothes thrown over the armchair in the corner of the room before stalking naked back to the bed. Reaching up, he pulled open the curtains so the lights from outside shone on the white sheets. And on Lily in her black lace dress, her skin shining pale beneath it. Even in the dim light he caught glimpses of the soft pink of her nipples and red-gold flash of the curls between her thighs. So fucking sexy.

Her eyes opened, her gaze dark as she stared up at him. Then her attention fell, moving down over his body and he let her look, enjoying the way her lips parted as she took him in.

"You didn't—" she began in a husky voice.

"No," he interrupted. "But there's a reason for that." He leaned over her, brushing the hair back from her face. "Are you okay? Do you hurt anywhere?"

"I don't think so."

"Good. Stay still now." He ran his hands down her legs, feeling the lithe, taut muscle of her thighs and calves, examining her just to make sure. "Do your feet hurt?" He'd take off her ballet shoes if they did but he liked them on her, especially the kink factor of fucking her with them on.

She shook her head, leaning back against the pillows and lifting her arms, her back arching like a cat being stroked. And he frowned, noticing something under her arm. A faint scar, standing out underneath the black lace. "Sit up. I want to take your dress off."

Obediently, she sat, lifting her arms, waiting while he pulled the dress up and over her head. Then he pushed her gently back down again, easing her left arm away from her body, running his fingers lightly over the scar near her armpit. She stiffened.

He flicked a glance at her, noting how the lines of her face had become guarded. "Where did you get that?"

Her hand came up and brushed his fingers away in what looked like a reflexive gesture. "It's nothing." She turned her head, not meeting his gaze.

Obviously it wasn't nothing.

He studied her shuttered face for a long moment. Something was going on with her, he could sense that much. Her stubborn, fighting spirit. The way she pushed. And then there was the strange way Rob treated her.

He let his fingers move lightly from the scar down over one small breast, cupping it in his hand, her nipple hardening responsively against his palm. She shivered and he heard her breath catch.

"You will tell me." He circled her nipple with his thumb, watching her face as a dart of pleasure crossed it. "I told you I wanted everything from you and I meant it."

"I…I thought you were only talking about sex."

"No." He pinched her nipple, watching as her lashes lowered, her pouty mouth opening on a sharp intake of breath. "I want your body *and* your secrets, ballerina. I don't want you holding anything back from me."

"Kahu—" His name ended on a low moan as he pinched her again, harder this time.

"You agreed. You're mine tonight and that includes everything about you, understand?"

But she shook her head. "Not this. Please."

No, he would not be merciful, not tonight. Because really, when would he ever have this chance again? When would another woman ever give herself to him freely? Willingly? Everything she was?

Probably never. Which meant this was the only night he'd ever have.

Releasing her, he got up from the bed, ignoring her surprised look.

Crossing over to the closet in the corner, he opened the door, bending to the drawer right down near the floor on the right. Where he kept certain pieces of equipment. Anita had given them to him years ago as a parting gift but he hadn't used them. He'd never felt the inclination.

Now though, it was time.

He gathered up a few items and carried them back to the bed, sitting down on the side and setting them out on top of the sheet for her to see.

She blinked. "What are those?"

"Some inducements. You're going to tell me what's going on, Lily. And these are going to help. I want you to choose one for me to use on you. If you continue to hold back, I'll add another but this time it'll be one of my choice."

Her gaze flickered away from his, and something shifted in his chest as he recognized it. Vulnerability. Shit, he didn't want to see that. It exposed vulnerabilities in himself he'd long forgotten, where he too had found out what it was like to be exposed.

No one should be without defenses, you prick. Especially not this twenty-year-old girl you're going to fuck then walk away from come morning.

He almost growled at the thought, not wanting it in his head. This was about *him* tonight, not about anything else. And it wasn't like he was going to harm her. If she wasn't getting off, he wouldn't. It was as simple as that.

"These are designed for pleasure," he said, giving her that at least. "Or to heighten it."

She glanced down at his little collection once more. "They look painful."

"Sometimes the pain can be a good pain."

"Oh sure. Is there ever good pain?"

"Yes definitely, there is."

She eyed him. "How do you know? Have you had these used on you?"

He didn't look away. "Yes."

"What? All of them?"

"Yes."

"And…?"

"It felt good. They all feel good if used right." This was another thing he was giving her, even though she didn't realize it. The things he'd done with his clients. With Anita…

There was curiosity in her gaze. "Where did you…um…who used them on you, I mean?"

"I was a rent boy, darling," he said. "Sucking cock wasn't the only thing I did."

"I'm sorry, I didn't mean—"

"I know you didn't. But you don't get to ask the questions tonight. I do."

She flushed. "Okay. I hear you. So I guess you know how to use them then."

"I do."

She shifted on the bed, folding her hands into her lap, staring down at the toys on the sheet. "What if I tell you everything now?"

He watched her face, studying her, wanting to think about her rather than what had happened in his past. He couldn't tell what she was thinking now and he wanted to. This whole thing was becoming less about a generalized someone and growing more specific to her by the minute. "Then we don't need to use any of these things."

She nodded, red-gold curls falling over her shoulder with the movement. "In that case…" Leaning forward, she picked up the vibrator. "I know what this is. I'm okay with it."

An odd sense of pride joined the satisfaction sitting in his gut. She may be as stubborn as hell but she was brave too and he liked that. "That's a good choice. But for the record, I'm aiming to use all of these on you tonight at some point."

Her eyes widened. "Not those." She gestured to the soft leather flogger and the nipple clamps. "Please."

"We'll see. But because you chose easily, I get to pick something."

"But—"

"Protest and I'll take that flogger to your backside."

She shut her mouth and it was amazing how good her instant obedience made him feel. The calm focus began to return, the anticipation building inside of him, and the determination. He would have this from her. He would.

Kahu picked up the handcuffs, the last remaining piece of equipment. "Hold out your hands."

She stared at them then lifted her gaze to his, and he could see the change and shift of her emotions. The fear warring with the desire. She wanted this but she'd never done it before and so she was afraid.

"You trusted me before, ballerina," he murmured, reminding her. "This is no different." He specifically didn't touch her now, wanting this from her willingly, no manipulations. And when she slowly put her hands out to him, he found his breath catching, his heartbeat loud in his ears.

He should say something, acknowledge her gift somehow, but he didn't know quite how. So instead he took each of her hands in his and turned her palms up, bent and kissed the center of each one. Then he snapped the handcuffs around one wrist.

She was looking at him, wide-eyed.

"Lie down," he said. "Hands above your head."

Slowly, she did so, allowing him to loop the handcuffs around the rail at the top of his iron bedstead and imprison her other wrist, clicking it shut.

He looked down at her, at the picture she made with her bright hair spilling over his pillows, her hands locked to his bed, pale and slender and achingly beautiful.

Yours.

That sense of satisfaction deepened. As if he'd been waiting for this moment for years, maybe his whole life. To have someone who was his, who'd given themselves up freely into his care, into his protection.

Jesus, it's like she sees more in you than just a broken down ex-prostitute.

Kahu ignored the voice. It didn't matter what he was or who he might once have been. What mattered was that Lily was his for the night and he was going to make sure she didn't regret that choice.

He would be hard on her to get what he wanted. He would push. But she wasn't going to get nothing out of this deal, he'd make sure of that.

Getting on to the bed, Kahu straddled her, his knees on either side of her hips. Her eyes widened as he did so but she didn't move, watching him. He leaned forward, putting one hand beside her head, looking down into her face and then at the scar under her arm. He ran a light finger down it, tracing it gently.

She shivered, her throat moving as she swallowed.

"What is this, Lily?" He traced it again. "How did you get it?"

"A tree scratched me when I was a kid."

He paused, studying her. She wasn't looking at him, her gaze off to the side beyond his shoulder. She was lying, he'd bet anything on it.

Slowly, he pushed himself back up and without a word reached behind him to pick up the flogger.

"Hey," Lily said thickly. "I didn't say you could—"

"You're lying to me, ballerina. So I'm adding another toy of my choice. And this is what I choose."

Her body had stiffened, her mouth open as she stared at the flogger in his hand. "Kahu, I don't think I—"

"It's okay, I'm not going to hit you with it." Pain wasn't the best thing to start off with right now, but getting her used to the toy wouldn't hurt. He bent over her again, trailing the leather ends across her breasts, hearing her breath catch. "Just a touch, sweetheart." He swept it over her again, the ends brushing across the scar. "It wasn't a tree, was it, Lily?"

She turned her head, her throat moving again. Goose bumps had started to come up all over her body, her nipples hard little berries. He shifted, trailing the leather farther down her stomach, over her thighs, between her legs. And she moved restlessly, the handcuffs rattling the rail as she did so.

"N-no, it wasn't," she admitted. She wasn't looking at him now, her attention on the flogger as he brought it back up her body, shivering again as the ends brushed over her pussy. Good, she was sensitive.

Kahu shifted again, pushing her knees apart before kneeling between her spread thighs. She took a ragged-sounding breath, the hands above her head curled into fists. Her eyes were dark and there was fear in them, but there was desire there too, battling it out with the fear.

"You're a fighter," he said softly, moving the flogger again, teasing her with it. "I can see you fighting with all your strength. Why, ballerina? What are you fighting so hard for?"

Her head turned, her hair falling over her face. "I don't want you to see me differently," she said thickly. "And if I tell you, you will."

He paused trailing the flogger. "What do you mean I'll see you differently?"

"If you know what that scar is. I'll change. I won't be...who you see now. I'll become someone different."

What the hell was she talking about? He leaned forward, pushed the hair away from her face and took her chin in his hand, turning her head so he could see into her eyes.

Yes, definitely fear. He didn't bother with the niceties. "Tell me, Lily."

Her lashes fell. "Okay. But don't...don't stop what you're doing. Please. I...like it."

He wasn't here for her. He was supposed to be here for himself. But that look in her eyes...that fear. He knew fear. Those first few months out on the streets of South Auckland, picking up clients, letting him do what they wanted to him in return for the money he took back to his family at night, he'd been terrified. He'd never gotten over that fear, but he'd learned to deal with it. Paper over the cracks of it so that no one knew.

He didn't expect her to feel it too, especially not here.

So he sat back, began to move the flogger over her body again, easing the leather over her nipples, circling them.

Lily's eyes fell shut. "It's a...biopsy scar." Her voice was ragged, thin. "From my lymph nodes."

A heavy stone settled on his chest. This wasn't going to be good, was it?

"When I was sixteen, I was diagnosed with acute, myeloid leukemia," she went on, the words sounding as if she was forcing them out. "I was in the hospital on and off for three years with chemo and a bone marrow transplant from which I had complications."

Leukemia. Fuck. *Fuck.*

The stone became a glacier, heavy as eons and twice as cold.

"I'm in remission now. But the treatment was hard and if you want to know why I fight that's why. Fighting is all I know how to do. Because if I didn't... If I stopped..." Her voice became shaky. "I was afraid I'd die."

He couldn't stop looking at her pale, finely carved face, the glacier moving slowly, crushing everything. He couldn't work out why he felt so intensely about this because after all, he hadn't known her long and it wasn't as if she was a lifelong friend or anything.

Maybe it was because of Anita, because he'd lost her too.

Lily was looking at him now and he could see the distress in her eyes. "See? I knew it, I knew you wouldn't look at me the same way. I'm a ghost to you too, aren't I?"

He couldn't deal with the enormity of the illness, of what she'd been through, so he focused on something else instead. Tossing aside the flogger, he leaned forward over her again, his hands beside her head. "What do you mean, 'a ghost to you too'?"

Her eyes were dark, the green vanished like leaves under ash. "It's stupid."

"Tell me, ballerina. I won't ask again."

She turned her head, red-gold lashes sitting still on her cheekbones. "Dad and I used to be closer. But when I got sick, it was like…I don't know, like he'd let me go already or something. He didn't visit me in the hospital, he didn't sit with me. He didn't talk to me." Her voice became thicker, rougher. "I was so afraid and he wasn't there. No one was there." Something seeped from underneath her lashes, glistening on her cheeks. Tears. "There was no one to give me a h-hug when I needed it. No one to hold my hand. No one to kiss me and tell me it was going to be all right."

It felt like she'd reached inside his chest, taken his heart in her hands and twisted hard. Rob, that fucker, had left her alone? While she was sick? Who the hell did that to their own daughter?

"And when I got better, when I moved home, he treated me like I was already gone. Like I'd died and come back as a stranger." Her chest heaved as she sucked in a breath. "All I want is for someone to hold me and tell me it'll be okay. Is that too much to ask? I'm so sick of fighting. I'm so sick of being afraid." The tears ran down her face. "And I miss my mother. I miss her kisses and her hugs. All I've had for years are needles and doctor's hands all over me, and I just want someone to touch me like there's nothing wrong with me. Like the leukemia never happened."

She turned her head away from him again, rubbing her cheek against the pillow, her voice choking. "I'm so fucking lonely and it hurts, Kahu. It hurts so much."

He couldn't speak. He knew that pain, knew it well. Because he felt it too. No one had touched him like that either. No one had held him or told him it would be okay. Not even his own mother. And that hadn't changed even when Anita had come. She'd touched him but it had only ever been about sex. There hadn't been anything emotional in her touches, nothing of comfort.

Sometimes being in bed with her had been the loneliest feeling on earth.

Kahu touched Lily's cheek, gently wiping away the tears, the wrenching pain in his chest twisting tighter. Nothing he could say was going to make this any better and he only knew of one way to ease the loneliness. It wasn't much. But it was all he had to offer her.

He bent, brushed his mouth over her salty skin, kissing away the tears. Then he kissed her lips, gently at first, tracing the soft curve of her bottom lip, nipping at her gently. She gave a groan, opening her mouth to him, lifting her head, and he could taste the hunger in her. Like his own. A hunger for a connection that went deeper than bodies meeting, deeper than the brief ecstasy of orgasm.

Her soul needed more than that and so did his.

So he opened his mouth to her, letting her explore him, her tongue at first tentative then becoming more confident, bolder. She tasted sweet, hot, so good.

He put his hand over her throat, stroking the graceful arch of it before sliding down to cup her breast, rubbing his thumb over her nipple. She moaned, arching up into his palm, the handcuffs rattling as she pulled against it.

After a moment though, he pulled away and sat up.

"No..." Her protest was desperate.

"Be still," he ordered, an idea taking shape in his head. "It's true, I do look at you differently. But not in the way you think. I don't see a ghost. I see the opposite. I see purpose and determination. I see pride. I see strength. I see a warrior, Lily. And I know you're tired, I know you want to rest. So lie back, ballerina. I'm going to show you how strong you can be when you surrender."

Chapter Eleven

She didn't understand him. How could there be strength in surrender? Especially now, naked and handcuffed to his bed. She felt like she'd had her soul removed from her chest and laid out for inspection. To be picked up and examined like all those doctors. Treating her like a disease not a person, deepening the isolation and loneliness that lurked in her heart like a canker, eating away at her.

Fuck, why had she said that? She hadn't expected it to all come rushing out. But there had been something about the feeling of leather on her skin, sensitizing her. About the heat of his body between her thighs. About the look in his dark eyes, like he was going to get this out of her one way or another.

And she'd known that he would. That she would end up telling him everything.

She didn't want to reveal it all. Didn't want to see the desire fade from his eyes because it wasn't like cancer was sexy. Didn't want him to know how lonely she was, how desperate for any kind of touch, any kind of connection. She hadn't known herself until it had all come tumbling out.

What a desperate, sad little person she was, and who wanted that? Certainly her father didn't.

Kahu had turned away, reaching for something on the bed behind him.

Her heart felt raw and painful, like it had been dragged on the ground behind a car. Her eyes were scratchy. All she wanted was to curl up in a ball, pull the covers up over her head and weep.

And then he turned back and she understood he wasn't going to let her. That far from fading, the desire that burned in his eyes now seemed to have a fierce purpose behind it.

He held the vibrator in his hand and the weird chain thing that had two little clamps on each end. Putting the chain down, he leaned over her, and her breath caught like it did every time he got close.

He was so hot in both senses of the word. When he'd first taken his clothes off, she thought she couldn't get enough of looking at him, because he was built like a god. Wide, powerful shoulders, his chest a wall of bronze skin and solid, heavy muscle. Lean waist and long, strong legs. A Maori tattoo, lots of black ink and graceful curves, climbed up one arm and over his shoulder, a piece of roughly carved greenstone on a flax cord hanging in the center of his chest. A stylized fishhook.

Gorgeous. Impossibly sexy.

Like now, leaning over her, all dark eyes and a fierce intensity that called her own to aching life. The smell of him and the heat of his body surrounded her and she had the weird impression that when she was with him, nothing could touch her. Not the cancer. Not the loneliness. Not the fear.

She was safe.

"I'm going to show you some things," he murmured, staring down at her. "And you may feel uncertain and you might want to say that word of yours."

Her throat felt thick and sore so she didn't speak, only nodded to show she understood.

"But you're not going to say that word, ballerina. You're going to lie there and show me how strong you are by taking what I give you, okay? And I'm going to give you pleasure. I'm going to show you that not all pain, not all loss of control is bad." He ran a hand down her side, a soothing touch that made her shiver all the same. "You might feel scared, but that's okay. You trust me to lead you, don't you?"

"Yes." The word came out on a croak.

"Good." Another long stroke. "Trust your body as well. It knows what it wants."

She swallowed, her mouth dry. "Okay."

His hand cupped her breast, his palm warm. Then he lowered his head and kissed her, at the same time pinching her nipple hard.

An intense bolt of sensation raced through her and she gasped against his mouth. The pinch hurt and yet she found herself aching, desire gathering in the pit of her stomach. He pinched her again, nipping at her lip and she shuddered. Then his hand slid down over her abdomen, moving down between her legs, the tip of one finger brushing over her exquisitely sensitive clit.

Lily jerked, gasping, the steel of the handcuffs hard against her wrists.

Kahu lifted his head and looked down at her and she had the impression he could see every part of her, every inch of her soul. "Are your hands okay? They haven't gone numb?"

"Yeah, they're okay… Oh…" The words ended on another gasp as his finger began to move in tight, concentrated circles around her clit, generating a flood of pleasure so sudden and intense it took her breath away.

"That's it," he murmured, his finger moving faster. "Take it, ballerina. Feel it."

Jesus, she couldn't help but feel it, the pleasure beginning to build fast and hard. She stiffened as it intensified. Too much too quickly and yet he didn't stop, his finger circling, teasing, forcing her higher.

The orgasm crashed over her without any warning, so tight and hard she had to close her eyes in a futile attempt to minimize the impact, her breathing hoarse, her body jerking helplessly in response.

Lights flashed behind her eyes as she lay there trying to figure out just what the hell had happened.

"Good girl." His voice was a purr. "You did beautifully." That teasing, taunting finger moved away and she felt his body shift on the bed.

Panting, she cracked open one eye. He was kneeling between her thighs, lifting something in his hands. She couldn't quite see what it was but when she felt something cool and smooth press against the opening of her body, she understood.

"No...please..." She moaned as he slid the vibrator gently into her. "I can't...it's too much." She felt pulled tight as a rubber band, as if any more sensation would make her snap.

"Yes, you can. You can take anything and everything I give you." He pushed her thighs apart wider, spreading the sensitive folds of her sex wider with his fingers, easing the toy in deeper. Then he switched it on.

Overloaded nerve endings screamed as pleasure crashed over them and she groaned, her hips jerking helplessly. "Kahu...I can't... Jesus..."

His hands stroked her forehead and down her neck, down over her shoulders. Soothing her, calming her. And then he cupped her breasts and pinched both nipples hard again. Lightning flashed between her sex and her nipples, a bright bolt of white-hot sensation. She let out a choked cry.

She'd never dreamed it was possible to feel this intensely, this completely. And despite the uncertainty and the fear, something hungry in her soul reveled in it.

It had been so long since she'd been touched, so long since she'd felt any kind of physical pleasure. Kahu's touch and the things he was doing to her were like rich food to a starving woman.

She couldn't resist, couldn't refuse. Oh she could say her word, but she didn't want to. Something in her craved all the sensation, as much of it as she could get, hoarding it for some long, cold winter.

"Keep your eyes closed, I think," he said softly. "And remember. This is for pleasure."

Then something cold pinched one nipple, a sharp pressure that didn't ease. And then the same pressure pinched the other nipple. She gasped, pain a bright thread weaving through the pulse of pleasure between her thighs.

"Kahu…" His name came out as a desperate croak.

"It's okay, ballerina. Breathe and remember the music. Don't fight it. Let it guide you. This pain is good, it won't harm you."

The pressure on her nipples was intense, the vibrations in her sex making her pant, making her jerk against the handcuffs around her wrists. Too much, too much.

His hands stroked her body, both soothing and inciting at the same time, down her hips and her thighs, caressing. A reassurance. Then she felt him take hold of the vibrator and begin to move it.

A sob caught in her throat, pleasure building like dark fire. And then, at the same time, she felt the pressure on her nipples increase, the pain sparking, joining the pleasure, becoming something more, something she'd never experienced in her entire life.

She arched, crying out, writhing helplessly. It felt like he was redrawing the pathways of her brain, rewiring them, showing her a new kind of sensation. Where pain was a variation on ecstasy, and pleasure, an exquisite kind of agony.

Where there was nothing but sensation, feeding the hunger that lived inside her, the yearning that had brought her to this point.

The world compressed, narrowed to encompass only the pressure on her nipples and the pulse of the vibrator between her legs. And Kahu's hands touching her, stroking her. Caressing her. Building and building the pleasure, layer upon layer, playing her body like an instrument. Making her sing. Making her fly.

Sparks flew behind her closed lids, stars glittered.

Someone was sobbing.

The pleasure/pain was the music she danced to, the air she breathed. It was her entire existence.

But in the end, her body could only take so much.

Lily screamed when the orgasm finally crashed down on her, complete as the world ending. Obliterating her consciousness, smashing her into pieces so small she was nothing but dust.

And afterwards she lay there while her soul returned to her, her heartbeat thumping and her pulse pounding. Burning steadily like a flame in the dark.

Kahu leaned over her, his heart pounding like a drum in his ear. She lay with her eyes closed, breathing fast and hard, her face wet with tears, red-gold curls stuck to her neck and forehead. He could see the aftershocks hit her in the tremble of her thighs and the movement of her breasts, the chain from the nipple clamps swinging slightly.

He couldn't seem to get a breath. Watching her take what he gave her and then scream from the pleasure of it had done something to him. The calm and the focus he'd had earlier seemed to have gone. Now he felt wild, out of control. Beside himself.

His hands shook and his cock was so hard it was painful and he had to have her. He just had to fucking have her now.

"You did so well, ballerina," he murmured roughly in her ear, reaching down between her thighs to remove the vibrator. "You're such a good girl."

She gave a little whimper as he slid the toy from her body then a groan as he gently uncuffed her and undid the nipple clamps, bending his head to lick the hard tips to soothe them.

She tasted of salt with a hint of vanilla that was all Lily, and he was suddenly completely desperate.

It was all he could do not to throw caution to the wind and push inside her immediately.

Fighting to find that calm again, Kahu reached for the nightstand drawer and the condoms in it. Keeping his movements slow and measured, he ripped open a packet and sheathed himself, his hands still shaking.

Fuck, what was wrong with him? He was never *this* desperate.

Leaning forward he gathered Lily into his arms, easing her into his lap so she was facing him, her skin damp and hot against his. "Are you ready for more?" He'd meant the question to sound soft, but it came out rough and far more ragged than he wanted.

"Yes." Her answer was barely more than a sigh and he could feel her tremble.

He wanted to ask her if she was sure but he simply couldn't wait. He felt like a rock climber on the edge of a mountain and about to fall, looking around desperately for something to hold on to before his hands slipped.

But there was only Lily.

He grabbed her hips, holding on tight, lifting her slightly before lowering her down onto him. She was so wet he slid in deep without any resistance, her body tight and hot around him.

"Oh…" The breath sighed out of her. "Kahu…" Her hair was falling all over her shoulders, her mouth full and delicious, the look in her eyes dark and smoky, and he still couldn't breathe. Couldn't move.

His grip on the edge of that mountain was slipping and he was going to fall.

Her hands lifted, cupping his face between her palms, her touch cool on his suddenly burning skin.

Now it wasn't only his hands shaking but his whole body too, and he didn't know the fuck why.

Her brow creased, her thumbs stroking along his jaw in an oddly tender motion. Then she bent and kissed him, lightly, delicately.

He shut his eyes because he couldn't keep looking at her anymore, not with that expression on her face, the one that made him feel as if he was twenty again and she was far older. Like she knew things he didn't.

Holding on tight, he flexed his hips, beginning to thrust up into her body. Hard. Deep.

"God…yes…." A soft moan then her hands sliding down his neck, stroking his throat, tracing the line of his collarbones, caressing his chest, his shoulders, his arms. Touching him like he was a wild animal she wanted to soothe.

And, fuck, he felt like a wild animal. This need, this desperation was spinning out of control, turning him into a beast driven only by instinct.

There was something about the lightness of her touch, the care implicit in it that made him feel raw, like she was stripping away a layer of skin, leaving him with nothing but nerve endings.

He didn't want light. He didn't want soothing. He wanted hard and rough. Violent.

With a growl, he changed positions, pushing her onto her back. Then he lifted her leg up and over his shoulder, her hips flexing with the movement, shoving himself deeper inside her. The breath hissed in her throat, her hands gripping his shoulders. But that look in her eyes was still there, the one that told him she knew what he was doing.

"Lily." Her name escaped without his permission.

She lifted a hand, touched his cheekbone then his mouth, tracing the shape of his lower lip. Gentle. So gentle. Touching him as if he wasn't dirty, as if he wasn't just an empty, broken-hearted whore.

He could feel something fracturing inside him, breaking like a crack in a pane of glass, spidering outwards.

Don't let her get close. Don't let her get near...

But it was too late. Far, far too late.

He was gasping, thrusting hard into her like he could crush the feeling inside him. Obliterate it with the sweetness of her mouth, the smooth skin of her body and the tight, wet heat of her cunt. Yet she kept touching him as he grew wilder, as the crack in his soul began to expand. Then he heard her gasp his name, feeling her sex contract around his cock, and it shattered completely.

Kahu buried his face in her neck as the orgasm descended like a hammer blow on the back of his head, splintering him like china, and he was shaking and shaking and shaking.

It felt like there was an air bubble in his chest preventing him from breathing. All he could do was lie there, the scent of her skin, flowers and sex, the heat of her body around him. Her hands moved on his back, stroking up and down his spine.

What the fuck just happened?

He had no idea. He'd never felt like this before during sex, not with anyone, even Anita.

Lily didn't say anything and he was glad because he didn't want to have to think of how to reply. Her fingertips trailed up and down, and he debated just lying there for the foreseeable future and not thinking. Not feeling anything but her fingers on his skin.

It was uncomfortable. Made him feel like with every pass she was taking off yet another layer of his soul.

If you let her keep doing this, you won't have anything left.

The thought was disturbing and he didn't know why.

Shifting away from her to get a bit of distance, he moved to get off the bed.

"Hey, are you okay?"

The question made him feel odd. Restless and not quite sure how to respond because he'd never been asked that question after sex before. Clients hadn't given a shit whether he was okay as long as they got off and sex with Anita had never been…

That raw?

"I'm fine," he said, closing that particular thought down, turning to smile at her to show her that there truly wasn't anything the matter. "I just need get rid of this condom."

"Oh." She rolled over onto her side. With her toes still in her ballet shoes, they pointed, making her look like she was dancing even lying down. "I know you said that this was all about you tonight, but can I make a suggestion?"

Christ. All about him… Yeah, he'd said that, hadn't he? How weird to think that when from the moment they'd walked through the door, it had been all about her.

"Sure. What?"

"This might sound weird, but can I have a bath?"

He didn't know why that should surprise him. Then again, everything she said seemed to surprise him, so why not this?

"I mean, you do have a tub, don't you?"

"Of course. I'll go run one for you."

She lay down flat on the bed, her chin resting on her folded hands. "It's big enough for two, right?"

It was. But he'd never had a bath with another person in it.

Sex. Keep it about sex. Don't think about the possibility of deep and meaningful conversation. About her hands touching you, caressing you. Stripping you bare…

"Yeah, it is. But if you're thinking of it being a relaxing option, I can pretty much guarantee that's not going to happen."

She flushed. "I'm good with that."

"In that case, why don't you wait here and get your strength back? I'll go start filling it up." He got off the bed and headed into the ensuite bathroom where the bath was, a big, clawfoot white enamel thing that took forever to fill.

Getting rid of the condom, he started the water running then went back out to the kitchen to get together some food and drink. Cheese and crusty bread and dip, some of the extra special fine, dark chocolate that Anita had given him a taste for. A bottle of French champagne.

"You're a sensualist, Kahu," she'd once told him. "You should indulge yourself more often than just sex."

She'd liked "spoiling him" as she'd termed it. And he let her because he'd never had any of the things she'd given him. He'd loved her and the thought of refusing her gifts had never crossed his mind, even when he didn't actually want some of them.

Not the food and drink, though, he liked that well enough.

When he got back to the bedroom, Lily was sitting on the side of the bed, her legs over the side. Her eyes lit up when he saw the tray he was carrying. "Oh my God, you read my mind. I'm starving."

The simple pleasure on her face was another crack in the wall he hadn't realized was there. He'd always liked looking after people, it was what had driven him onto the streets in the first place, wanting quick money after his gang-patched father had gone to jail for assault. His mother couldn't get a job and with four younger siblings all needing to be fed and a roof kept over their heads, it had seemed the easiest way. Certainly to his sixteen-year-old way of thinking it had looked less dangerous and violent than running drugs for his father's gang.

Pity it didn't end up being that simple.

No, it hadn't. He'd been naïve. Stupid. Hadn't realized how terrifying it had been to give another person control over your body. To let them do things to you that you didn't like and wouldn't have chosen if there had been another way.

But no, he wasn't going to be thinking about that. It was the decision he'd made and he couldn't unmake it.

Coming over to the bed, he set the tray down and put the bottle and the two glasses he'd also been holding onto the nightstand.

"Can I take these off now?" Lily pointed one slender, ballet shoe-covered foot.

Kahu glanced down at it. Well, he'd indulged his little fetish for the time being, and if they hurt her, he definitely didn't want her keeping them on. "I think so. But since I put them on, I'll take them off." He knelt, took her foot in his hand and began undoing the ribbons. "They really hurt?"

"Yeah. But it's okay. Dance is pain." There was a small, ironic smile turning her mouth. "And it turns out I'm pretty good at dealing with pain."

"So you are." He began to untie the ribbons, unwinding them from around her narrow ankle. "I guess you've had practice."

She sighed. "Tell me about it. Nothing like cancer to test your pain threshold."

He slid off her shoes, noting the bruises on her toes and the cracked nails. Apparently she was telling the truth about dance being pain. He stroked the sensitive hollow behind her ankle and looked up, studying her face. "You were in the hospital a long time."

"It was a long time. I had complications with my treatment, stuff like that."

"What happened with your dancing?"

Her full, pouty mouth tightened. "Nothing, that's what happened. Cancer pretty much screwed my career. That's why I'm trying to get this audition. I'm trying to make up for the three years I lost."

Three lost years. A long time for a young dancer. A long time for a sixteen-year-old girl who should have been at school enjoying her life with friends and boyfriends and parties and all that kind of shit.

"You have to do it now? You can't sit back and enjoy life for a bit?"

She frowned. "No. I don't have time. A ballet career starts young. I mean, all the other girls I knew are dancing overseas already. If I want a career, I have to do this now before I'm too old."

Christ. Too old at twenty. "Life is more than just ballet, sweetheart."

Abruptly, she looked away. "Yeah, well, it may be for other people. But I don't have anything else. I had to focus on something to get me through the cancer and ballet was it."

"Come on, you don't have any other interests? Or friends?"

"No," she said dully. "For the past three years I've been trying not to die, so I didn't have time to develop any other hobbies."

I'm so fucking lonely, Kahu…

He didn't want her to be lonely. He didn't want her to be in pain. He could see himself in her, the teenager lost to the streets. Who'd eventually been kicked out of his home when his father had gotten out of jail and found out how his oldest son had been keeping the family alive.

Both he and Lily had had something taken from them. An essential part of themselves.

The crack in the wall inside him widened, getting larger.

"You have me," he said before he could stop himself. "I'll be your friend."

The tightness around her mouth relaxed and she smiled, full-on and bright, an unexpected gift. "Yeah? I'd like that."

Bits of the wall were crumbling now, like bricks under a wrecking ball.

Fuck's sake, stop.

He looked away, his heart pounding, busying himself with the ribbons on the other shoe. "I have lots of hobbies I can introduce you to." He pulled at the knot. "Drinking French champagne in the bath, for example. The number of orgasms it's possible to have in an hour. How many shots of scotch you can have before you fall over."

Shut the fuck up, you idiot. You're babbling.

Cool fingers slid over his own at her ankle. "Kahu?"

He didn't look up, staring at her pale hands over his. "What?"

"Are you okay?"

No. You're not okay.

Gently he shook her hands away and finished with the knot. "What makes you say that?" He unwrapped the ribbons and slid her shoe off, trying to mask the fact that his fucking hands were still shaking.

"You seem...I don't know...nervous or something."

He placed the shoe on the ground. "Sure. I'm worried about the bath overflowing. Hang on while I just go check it."

Liar. Liar. Liar.

He got up and walked back into the bathroom, checking on the water level then turning the tap off before leaning against the white porcelain vanity and closing his eyes.

He didn't know what she was doing to him, because it was definitely something she was doing. Out of all the women he'd had in his bed, she was the only one who was getting to him. Like a sapper digging a tunnel beneath the castle walls, she was undermining some part of him that needed to stay strong.

To keep people out, right?

Soft footsteps. The scent of flowers and musk. "Kahu?"

He opened his eyes and found Lily standing in front of him, naked and beautiful, a look of concern on her face. "Something's wrong, isn't it?" She lifted a hand to cup his cheek.

"Don't touch me." The words broke from him before he could stop them, a harsh sound. And the instant he'd said it, he regretted it.

Her eyes widened, a spark of hurt flaring in them, and her hand dropped. "I'm sorry. I didn't mean to pry."

Already he could feel the side of his face aching from the lack of contact. Almost as if his soul was yearning for the connection. Was hungry for it.

She will break you if you let her.

And she would. Those cracks kept running through him and with every touch, with every glimpse of her brave, determined spirit, they just kept deepening, widening. He didn't want to know what would happen if the wall crashed down. Something terrible. Something he didn't want to face.

But he also didn't want to hurt her. And he had.

"No," he said harshly, suddenly furious with himself. "I'm sorry. But you should know I'm not up for any heart-to-heart chats, okay?"

Her expression shuttered. "I wasn't asking you for heart-to-heart chats. I just wanted to know if you were okay. But hey, clearly you are, so forget I asked." She began to turn away.

Fucking hell, he was ruining this.

Reaching out, he grabbed her arm, turning her back to him. "I'm sorry, Lily. I didn't mean to snap at you."

Anger simmered in her eyes. "I thought you said you were going to be my friend. Or didn't you mean it?"

"I did mean it… Christ." He pushed his hand through his hair, feeling out of his depth. He didn't want to tell her anything, reveal himself, and yet he hated the thought of hurting her. "I just don't like talking about myself very much."

"I only asked if you were okay. I didn't want your life story or anything."

No, she hadn't. And she'd given him hers in the bargain.

Don't tell her. Keep yourself safe.

Her skin under his fingers on her arm was warm and soft, and it didn't take much pressure to pull her closer, to get that warm, soft skin up against his. The breath hissed out of her in a little rush as he slid an arm around her waist, his palm curving over her butt, fitting the hot, damp heat of her pussy against his hardening cock.

Yeah, this was it. This was all there ever was. Heat and slick flesh and hungry mouths. Like good food or fine wine, a brief spark of physical pleasure in the darkness. He *was* a sensualist. And why not? It was a damn sight better than any kind of emotional crap that was for sure.

Maybe that was the key. Bring it back to why they were here. Sex and control. Nothing more.

"Just as well. My life story would make for depressing reading." He bent his head and brushed her mouth with his, coaxing her lips to open. Sliding his tongue in to taste her. "Now," he murmured after a moment. "Like I said, you're here for me and what I want is your ass in that bath."

Yet Lily had stiffened in his arms and when he raised his head, he saw that the anger in her eyes hadn't faded. It was burning there still.

"Ballet," she said.

Chapter Twelve

His jaw hardened as she said the word, but she didn't look away and she didn't back down. His body was hot against hers and all she wanted to do was press herself against it, but she wasn't going to do that either.

She didn't have a lot of experience with friendship, but she did know it was about give and take. And that she didn't want to be the one doing all the taking, she wanted to give as well. Especially to him. Whatever he'd done with that pain/pleasure thing had been incredible, like he'd reset her somehow. The experience of the leukemia would always be there and he hadn't wiped it away just like that, but something inside her felt easier, as if a pressure had been released. And now she wanted to do the same for him, except he seemed hell-bent on preventing her.

Well, shit. She'd learned about surrender from him, but this wasn't about surrender. Now was the time to fight.

"Ballet, huh? You're playing a mean game, little girl." The anger in his eyes was swiftly masked and an offhand, casual note entered his voice. "And your damn bath is going to get cold." Releasing her, he eased her away from him.

Lily folded her arms, shivering at the sensation across the tips of her sensitive nipples. She felt cold and really wanted that bath, but she wasn't going to back down here.

She didn't know why he'd gone all weird when she'd tried to touch him. She didn't know why he'd gone all weird now—she could feel the distance he was putting between them—but one thing was certain: she was bloody well going to find out.

Her main problem was trying to get through that jaded, cynical wall he kept throwing up when she pushed him. And she was sure it was a wall and that he was using it to protect himself.

You're going to ruin this if you're not careful.

She might and if she wanted an easy life, doing what he said and getting in that bath were the best way to get it. But she couldn't leave this alone. There was more to Kahu Winter than the jaded, cynical man she'd come to know, she was sure of it. And she wanted to find out what more there was.

"I don't care," she said, lifting her chin. "I want to know why you didn't want me to touch you."

His eyes were opaque and blacker than obsidian. "Sorry, sweetheart, but I don't have to explain myself to you."

"You don't. I thought you might like to, though, seeing as how you were quite happy for me to touch you not five minutes ago."

"Jesus. Okay, we'll do it your way." He pushed her gently against the side of the tub. "Sit down and let Uncle Kahu tell you a story."

The enamel was cold but colder still was the irritation on his face. And the boredom. "What story?"

"Since I'm clearly not going to get to fuck you until your curiosity is satisfied, I am now going to satisfy it. And then you're going to get into that bath and onto my cock. Are we clear?"

She narrowed her gaze. Oh he was definitely protecting himself, the way he always did with shocking words issued in that voice redolent with manufactured boredom. The armor he wore to keep the world at bay.

"Crystal," she said. "But let's also agree that I didn't ask you for this. You wanted to give it to me."

Another lightning flash of anger moved through his eyes then it was gone. "Yeah, whatever. Consider it a present." He backed away to lean against the vanity, the cold light of the bathroom shining over the bronze skin of his abs and the heavy plane of his chest. He was still hard and standing there, looking down at her, he seemed like a kind of warrior god. Powerful, strong, intensely masculine.

Hell, he was such a beautiful man. Was she mad to push him like this when she could be in the bath right now? In the warm water with his arms around her, his cock inside her, giving her so much pleasure?

Yeah, you're fucking crazy.

Lily hardened her jaw, keeping her arms folded. And waited.

"Here's the facts, ballerina," he said, his voice uninflected. "My dad was a gang member and when I was sixteen, he went back to jail for the fourth time for assault. My mother had no money, no qualifications, nothing but the benefit. And I had four other siblings. We had to find some cash to keep everyone fed and pay the damn rent otherwise we'd be out on the streets. Dad wanted me to be a gang prospect but I hated them. They were murdering scum and I wanted nothing to do with them. I didn't have any qualifications and since I left school at fifteen, no damn education either. I had two choices, running drugs or stealing." He shifted against the vanity, his hands behind him, fingers gripping onto the white porcelain. "I hated either of those choices. Both were dangerous and if I got caught I'd go to jail too. Then I noticed a mate of mine had this fancy new jacket. He had no money so I asked him where he'd got it. He wouldn't tell me. Eventually though, after a lot of beer, he told me he'd been sucking the dicks of rich, *pakeha* guys. It was easy, over in five minutes and he got cash for it."

Lily's chest felt hollow. She tightened her arms, holding the feeling inside. The look in his eyes was full of a kind of fatalism that made the hollow feeling even worse, but she didn't look away. If he could bear to tell it, she could bear to listen.

"I wasn't gay," Kahu went on. "But it sounded like easy money to me and we fucking needed it. So my mate told me where to go and what to do and that's what I did. Turns out it wasn't as easy as I thought, at least the first time wasn't." The shadows of memory lingered in his eyes, a flicker, then vanishing. "But after that, it wasn't so bad. I managed to keep the family in cash while Dad was in jail for at least a couple of years. And then he got out and came home and found out what I'd been doing. He was fucking furious. He beat me to within an inch of my life and threw me out of the house."

She almost flinched at his casual tone. The hollow feeling intensified and she had to grit her teeth.

Kahu's posture was relaxed, like he was relating a story that had happened to someone else, someone who wasn't him. He even smiled at her, a smile that didn't reach his eyes. "Too difficult for you, love? I told you it made for depressing reading."

"Oh no, don't stop," she said sarcastically. "It's just getting good."

The fake smile turning his mouth eased fractionally. "So after I'd recovered from dear old Dad's little display of love, I obviously couldn't go home. I went into the inner city instead, lived on the streets for a while. Turned tricks on the side. You know the bridge over Grafton Gully? I lived under there. Great place. Lots of atmosphere. Indoor-outdoor flow, the works."

"Kahu," she said.

Unexpectedly he glanced away for a moment and when he looked back, all the amusement was gone from his voice. From his face. He looked hard. Cold. A god of anger. "And then some fucker stole Anita's purse and I got it back and gave it to her. And she invited me back to this bar for a drink to thank me. She bought me a glass of wine—I'd fucking never had wine in my life—and we talked. All night. She wanted to help me, she said, and asked me to meet her for coffee the next day. I did. Eventually she offered me a place to stay. Food. A proper bathroom. She helped me go back to school, get some decent qualifications. She even got me into law school, though that wasn't my thing so I dropped out." His jaw tightened, the hard, cold gleam in his eyes becoming even harder. "She took me overseas, she showed me the world. Gave me a taste of all this stuff I'd never even thought existed. For five years I lived with her, shared her bed and her life. Then she told me she had Huntington's disease, that she was going to be very sick and eventually it would kill her. Then she cut me off. Told me our relationship was over."

Lily blinked, her throat dry and tight. Beneath the hard note in his voice she could hear the pain. God, this woman who'd saved him from the gutter then cut him off? Just like that? "Why?" she forced out.

"I don't know. I told her I was in love with her, that I wanted to marry her. But she said I didn't know what I felt. That I didn't love her and she didn't love me so it was a moot point." A muscle jumped in his jaw. "Anyway, long story short, she left me the club as a goodbye present or some such shit, while I left the country for five years. When I came back to Auckland, she was in a nursing home and the illness had advanced. I visited her every week, read to her." There was the smallest pause. "She died six months ago."

Again, there was no obvious change in his tone but Lily could hear it. Could see the glint of it in his eyes. Anger. Pain. Grief.

"Why?" she repeated. "Why did you visit her? After she chucked you out like that?"

He shifted again. "I loved her, sweetheart. I couldn't leave her slowly dying in a home without at least one visit."

She stared at him. "You're angry with her, though."

Surprise passed over the brutally handsome lines of his face then he laughed, a strangely empty sound. "Angry with her? Yeah, well, I was. Once. It's all water under the bridge now, though. She's dead. End of story." He pushed himself away from the vanity and came around the side of the bath, gestured to it. "In."

But it wasn't the end of the story. Somehow Anita still had a hold on him, she was sure of it. All that anger and pain and grief had to come from somewhere. Had it been from the horror of his early life or was it all Anita? Then again... The shock of it, a prostitute from the streets suddenly brought into the life of a rich, sophisticated woman. He must have thought he was entering the kingdom of heaven and Anita the goddess.

She swallowed. "That still doesn't explain why you didn't want me to touch you, though."

"Oh for fuck's sake." Unhidden anger glittered in his gaze. "You don't want to get in the bath? Fine. I don't force anyone to do what they don't want and I don't manipulate either. But darling, if you don't want another screw then it's probably better you go home. Understand?"

It would have hurt if she hadn't known that his defense mechanisms were kicking in. That he was trying to keep the distance between them.

Abruptly she remembered being in his arms as he'd held her on the bed, sliding inside her, the pleasure of it overwhelming. And she'd felt half drunk, dizzy with desire, unable to stop touching him. Smooth skin and sweat and densely packed muscle. She'd wanted to learn every inch of him, stroke and caress him like the beautiful man he was. But she remembered the look on his face, the strange hint of fear in his eyes. He'd shook then pushed her onto her back, aggressive and hungry.

Another memory. His hands shaking as they'd undid the ribbons on her ballet shoes.

Was that her? When she was trying to close the distance between them?

That's why he didn't want you to touch him...

Kahu was getting into the bath, the water displacing as he sunk his large body into it. He sat at the other end to where she was perched, a weary, cynical expression on his face. "Well? What's it to be? Another screw or are you finding your own way home?"

"I know what you're doing," she said quietly. "You're trying to push me away."

He raised a brow. "Oh, and you think you know me well enough to comment, sweetheart?"

"Does anyone know you well enough to comment, Kahu? Did Anita?" It was a guess, but she saw it hit home in another flare of barely hidden anger that glittered in his eyes. "Or did you use the same tactic with her? The stupid, meaningless endearments. The 'I'm a jaded cynical manwhore' bullshit?"

His mouth flattened into a hard line. "Get into the bath, little girl. Or get your ass out of here. I'm not going to say it again."

Lily's heart began to beat fast, her mouth drying. This was a gamble and if she played wrong, she'd probably never see him again. But shit, this was important and so was he. And if she had any hope of continuing this beyond another night, she had to win this round.

You want to continue this beyond another night?

Shoving the thought away, Lily slipped off the side of the bath. "Okay," she said. "If that's the way you feel."

Then she turned and walked out of the bathroom.

Every muscle in Kahu's body tightened in instinctive reaction as Lily turned on her heel in a flare of silky red-gold curls and walked out.

Why did she always do that? Why did she *always* do the thing he didn't expect her to do?

Oh come on, you really expected her to jump into the bath with you after that?

His jaw was so tight it felt like it was going to crack.

Fuck her. Let her go. Let her walk. He didn't care. He'd told her about his sordid past—it wasn't a fucking secret after all—and if she couldn't get past that then too bad.

Yet desire and anger and a sharp, barbed pain sat in his gut.

You don't want her to go.

He gripped onto the edge of the bath, listening to the sounds of her in the bedroom. But there was nothing. Had she gone already? A thump. Fuck, was that the front door shutting?

Let her go. Protect yourself.

But he was moving before he was even aware of doing so, propelled by a need he hadn't realized had grown so large. A yearning he couldn't quite suppress no matter how hard he tried.

With a surge of water, Kahu got out of the bath and strode, dripping wet, out of the bathroom.

She wasn't there.

Fuck. Fuck. Fuck.

He went out and down the short hallway and came out into the lounge in time to see her on the point of opening the front door. She was dressed already, her satchel slung over her shoulder.

"Lily, stop." He didn't wait for her to reply or respond, he continued walking as she turned to face him, coming right up to her and reaching out, pulling her hand off the door handle. Putting one hand on her hip and pushing her up against the closed door. Pinning her to it, heedless of the fact that he was wet and she was dressed.

She looked up at him, her stubborn jaw set, her eyes full of determination. She didn't move or struggle, just stood there, stiff as a board. Waiting while he stood there naked and hard and sick with wanting.

Anger, thick and hot flooded through him. He put a hand on her throat, the slender bones so fragile against his palm. Her pulse was racing, as fast as his.

"Is this another game, sweetheart?" he demanded. "Another tactic to get me to do what you want?"

A hot, green spark glinted in her eyes. "Why do you think I'm playing games with you every time I try and get close? All I want is some honesty, Kahu. That's all I want."

"I was honest with you. I told you all about—"

"That's shit. You gave me a collection of facts about your life. That's not honesty."

He could feel his pulse getting out of control. Fuck, this whole situation was getting out of control. He should be letting her go, letting her walk. But he couldn't seem to do it. Couldn't seem to stand back and let her go.

She was warm and smelled of flowers and musk and he wanted her arms around him. He wanted her to touch him like he wasn't dirty or broken. He wanted her so badly.

"I didn't promise you honesty." He couldn't keep the edge of desperation from his voice. "We're not in love, darling. We're fucking. For one night and one night only. That's all it is. And you don't need honesty for that."

But the look on her face was unyielding. "Yeah, well, you may not need it. But I think I do. You told me you'd be my friend, Kahu. And friends are honest with each other."

"How would you know? You told me you don't have any friends." The harsh words spilled out helplessly. Even now he couldn't seem to give her what she wanted. Even now when all he wanted to do was pull her close, something else seemed determined to keep her away.

Hurt filled her eyes, her chin jutting. "I thought I had you, at least. Guess not." She gave him a little shove. "Let me go. I need to get out of here."

Prick. You fucking prick.

Yeah, he was a prick. He was dirty and broken and all of that shit. And he knew he should move, let her leave. But he didn't.

"You're right," he said hoarsely. "I am angry with Anita. I wanted her to love me but she never did. She sent me away instead, giving me this fucking club as some sort of consolation prize. Payment for services rendered."

Lily said nothing but she didn't take her gaze from his.

"And when I came back to Auckland, I went every Thursday to read to her. So she would know that I came back for her. That I didn't leave her. That I was still here no matter what she said." The anger rose up inside him, bitter and frustrated, burning like acid. "I thought I was worth something to her. I thought that when she took me into her home, into her life, when she gave me all these things, that it was because I was worth it. But you know what? I wasn't worth shit to her. I was still just a fucking rent boy." He was shaking again. How bloody ridiculous.

Lily didn't move and she didn't touch him, and he wanted her to so much. She only looked at him, with that sharp, perceptive stare. And the words kept coming.

"She gave me all this stuff I didn't even want. Art tours and opera and literature. Jesus, to a street kid from South Auckland it was almost inconceivable. And she never asked me if I wanted it or not, she just did it. I was her project, that's all I was. I was being remade into who she thought I should be, not what I was."

"And who is that?" she asked quietly.

He went still, staring down into her finely carved, delicate face. Who he was? Well, fuck, that was easy, wasn't it? He was a poor, uneducated Maori boy, trying to help his family. A kid with no job and no prospects. Who'd whored himself out for money.

"Nobody," he said, his voice fraying and coarse as old linen. "I was nobody."

Something fierce crossed her face. "No. You're not nobody, Kahu." And at last she reached up her hand and touched his face. Her cool fingers so light, as if she was touching his soul and didn't want to break it. "You're somebody. You're somebody amazing."

It hurt, that touch. And all he was able to manage was a couple of moments, even though he wanted it with all of his being. But he couldn't afford it. She *would* break him and he couldn't break. Couldn't hand over that final piece of himself. He didn't have a lot of it left after Anita.

Crap. You kept that piece from Anita too.

He ignored the snide thought, taking Lily's wrist in his fingers and gently pulling it away. Then, still gentle, he lifted her wrist beside her head and pinned it to the door behind her. She did nothing, motionless as he did the same with her other hand, his finger imprisoning her, holding her there.

He bent his head, brushed her mouth with his, inhaling her scent, feeling the slender, tensile strength of her body against him. "I don't want to talk anymore, ballerina. All I want is one more time with you. Please. Give that to me."

Her wrists flexed against his imprisoning fingers and he heard the breath catch in her throat. "Only on one condition."

He let his mouth trail down her throat, tasting the salt on her skin. If he closed his eyes, he could lose himself in her and right at this particular point in time, he couldn't think of anything better. "What?"

"You let me touch you the way I want to."

Slowly, he lifted his head. Her skin had flushed, her eyes glittering with the same passion that was burning in him. But her determination was just as strong. She'd leave if he didn't give her what she wanted, no doubt about that.

So what? Let her go. You can find someone else.

Yeah, he could. Downstairs, in the club right now he would find many women he could bury himself inside of. A brief meaningless encounter that would relieve this nagging ache.

An encounter that wouldn't touch either of them.

But he was beginning to think that perhaps he wanted to be touched. Needed a connection that was real, that was genuine. Where there were no walls. Only themselves.

And he didn't want that with just anyone. He wanted that with Lily.

Lily, who now held more of him than anyone ever had. Even more than Anita.

Brave, stubborn, surprising, vulnerable Lily.

Kahu let her wrists go and stepped back. Her eyes widened and he felt a brief surge of satisfaction that he hadn't lost the power to surprise her in return. "Touch me then," he said.

A flush tinged her cheeks. Unhooking the satchel from around her narrow shoulders, she dropped it on the floor. Then she took a couple of steps, closing the distance he'd put between them.

He made himself stand motionless, waiting for her. His skin was still damp but he wasn't cold. No, he was hot. Ready to burn.

She stepped right up to him and put her hands on his chest and even that small touch was like a match to paper, setting him alight. Her gaze was on his chest, following the movements of her hands as she stroked him. Collarbones, chest, abs. Light, tantalizing touches. Her searching fingers found the ink on his skin, tracing it. "Where did this come from? It's beautiful."

He had to take a breath and close his hands into fists to stop them from reaching for her, stripping her of her clothes and thrusting into her, anything so this ache would stop.

"I got it after I left Anita. To remind myself of where I came from. Not the gangs and shit, deeper than that. My mother's people." Another piece of himself he didn't have to give away to anyone. A piece of himself that remained permanently inked into his skin.

Her fingers followed the swirling lines. "See?" she murmured. "You are someone."

His throat closed up, and more than anything he wanted to pull her hands away from him. But he didn't. He closed his fists tighter instead.

"What about this?" She lifted the piece of greenstone on his chest, examining it.

"Anita gave it to me when I left." *When she kicked you out.* "Greenstone can only be given, not bought."

"Yeah, so I heard. What does the fishhook mean?"

"It's…supposed to be a symbol of being a provider. A hunter."

She let it fall back onto his chest, the weight of it suddenly heavy. "You kept it."

"You can't give those kinds of gifts away or sell them." No matter how angry you were. No matter how heartbroken.

Sure you were heartbroken. Or maybe you were only angry?

"No, I guess you can't." Her fingers moved lower, over his abs again, down even farther, and when her fingers brushed the head of his cock, the breath hissed in his throat. An impossible touch.

She looked up at him, a crease between her brows. And for some reason that slightly quizzical look combined with the tantalizing circling of her fingers around the head of his dick made him feel suddenly, utterly desperate.

"Lily." Her name sounded almost strangled and he couldn't stop it. "Please."

"I want to give you something." Her fingers circled again. "Something that's for you."

"Just keep doing that and I'll be extremely fucking happy."

The crease deepened. "No, that's not it." Her hands dropped and she stepped back from him abruptly. He almost groaned, almost reached to drag her back.

"Wait here," she said and walked past him toward the bedroom.

Wait here? What the fuck?

He turned around and a couple of seconds later she was coming back, this time carrying something in her hands.

The flogger.

His heart went still. Everything in the entire world went still.

"You said you wanted to use this on me," she said and held it out to him. "But you haven't yet, not really."

He didn't take it, not immediately, looking at her face instead. Her expression was full of that fierce determination and resolution that was part of her nature. "Lily…I thought you didn't want me to."

"I know. Well, I've changed my mind."

"Why?"

"I told you. I wanted to give you something. So I'm going to give you this."

"Lily—"

"Well? Do you want it or not?" She shook her hand at him, the leather ends of the flogger swinging. "You understand, right? I'm trusting you. You told me it would be good and you've already shown me that pain doesn't have to be bad. So I'm trusting you to keep your word. To make it good for me."

He didn't know what to say. No one had ever given him this. He'd always been on the receiving end when it came to some of the sexual games clients played, and as for his other lovers, none of them had ever put themselves in his hands so completely.

Certainly Anita had never done so. For all her liberalism, she'd been quite a conservative lover and he'd always had the feeling that was his fault. She'd never let go with him, not once.

You can't take this. You can't have her.

But she was looking at him with so much of that fierce determination in her eyes. And naked need. And hope. A combination even more arousing and intense than the softness of her touch.

He knew what it was like to have that kind of gift thrown back in your face. He couldn't refuse this.

Slowly, he reached out and took the flogger from her, the handle cool against his palm. "Are you sure you want this, ballerina? It will hurt."

She just looked at him, measuring and far too sharp. "Are you sure you want to give this to me?"

He couldn't give her back anything but the truth. "No, not really."

"Then that makes two of us." Her chin lifted. "So where do you want me?"

You're really going to do this?

Yeah, it seemed he was. And the prospect of showing her how good this could be, of how intensely he could make her feel, was already making the anticipation gather tight inside him.

His grip firmed on the handle of the flogger. "Over the arm of the couch, I think."

She did as she was told, walking over to the couch and positioning herself over one arm, her body curving gracefully. Slowly, he followed her, waiting until she was ready, her hands braced on the couch cushions. She wore her black lace dress and there was something appropriate about it, about how she was dressed while he was the one naked.

He certainly felt naked, though it had nothing to do with the fact that he wasn't wearing anything and more to do with the raw sensation building in his gut. A combination of desire, need and fear. And especially the last, he couldn't work out. Because he was the one in control, the one with the power.

Yet looking at her bent over the couch, waiting for the lash to fall, trusting him to make it good for her, made him feel afraid. Stripped him completely bare.

It was the most exposing thing he'd ever had to do, and yet he wasn't able to walk away.

Instead he put down the flogger so he could ease up her dress, reveal the pale length of her legs, the curve of her ass. Then he tugged down her panties, pushing them down her thighs and as he did so, he could feel her tremble.

His mouth was dry, his heart pounding. Gently, he ran his hands over her buttocks, stroking her, calming her. "It's okay," he murmured, the feel of her skin beneath his palms like warm silk. "You have your word, remember? You can say it whenever you want."

"I know." Her voice was muffled.

He let his fingers trail down the backs of her thighs, sliding his fingertips between them, brushing the soft folds of her pussy, her breath catching audibly as he did so. He began to play with her, circling around the entrance to her body before sliding a finger into her heat, testing her. She was damp, but not quite wet enough for him yet. He wanted her aroused and panting on the edge before he brought pain into the mix.

She gave a soft sigh as he caressed her, but her body was tense. Not what he wanted. He sank to his knees behind her, stroking up and down her thighs. "Legs apart for me, ballerina."

She widened her stance obediently and he slid his hands up her legs so he could grip her hips, tugging her back a little so she was bent forward even more. Then he reached up and parted the folds of her pussy, opening her up like a flower and tasting her.

Lily gasped and he could feel the nervous tension start to bleed out of her, to be replaced by a different kind. He pushed his tongue inside of her at the same time as he slid a hand forward, finding and stroking the hard bud of her clit. Timing the push of his tongue with the touch of his finger. She made another, choked sound.

He closed his eyes, every sense he had focused on the salty, tart taste of her, the delicate musky scent of sex, the feel of her body, all wet flesh and tight, grasping heat. Her thighs had begun to tremble, her moans ragged. She began pushing back against him, demanding more.

Kahu slowed, tantalizing her. He wanted to bring her to the peak before that leather went anywhere near her. Wanted her nearly at the edge, when her pain threshold would be higher, let her be able to cope with it. And he should know, he'd had it done to him more than once.

Eventually, he felt her body begin to tense and shake, her orgasm just within reach. He pulled away and straightened.

"No," she moaned. "Don't stop."

He picked up the flogger, stroking her pale skin. "I'm not stopping." Fuck, he sounded as ragged as she did. And he kind of was. His head was full of her taste and smell, and he wanted nothing more than to have her right now. But his control was rigid and he wouldn't. Not yet, Christ, not yet.

He had to prove to her that her trust wasn't misplaced. That she'd given him a gift and he would accept it. He wouldn't throw it away like it meant nothing to him. Because it did. It meant…so much.

Kahu raised his arm. And brought the leather down on her pale skin.

She cried out, her fingers clutching instinctively onto the couch cushions, her body stiffening. He didn't give her any chance to adjust or anticipate, bringing it down on her again, the sound of it hitting her flesh echoing in the room.

Another cry, redness beginning to appear on her skin. He brought it down again, and a fourth time. Her whole body was shaking now, the sounds she made thin and reedy. He put a hand on her back, letting her know he was there and lowered the flogger, ready to hear if she wanted to say her word or not.

She didn't, her sides heaving.

He stroked her back gently then slid his palm over her butt, soothing the redness. She groaned as he did so, shivering and panting.

Kahu let his hand trail between her thighs again, testing her. And yeah, Jesus, she was so wet. He played with her a little bit more, easing a finger into her, before leaning over and pushing her hair away so he could see her face.

She was deeply flushed, her mouth open, her eyes closed. Her expression twisted with agonized pleasure as he slid his finger deeper and the breath he'd been holding for what seemed like ages suddenly released.

"You like this, don't you?" he whispered, adding another finger. "I can feel how you like it. This pain is good pain."

"Yes…so good." Her voice was rough. "Please, Kahu…please…"

But no. He wouldn't give it to her just yet. He wanted this to be intense, amazing. He wanted to make sure she'd never regret giving him this.

He eased his fingers out of her and picked up the flogger again, administering a few more blows. Not hard but not holding back too much either, so she was squirming and shivering, her cries hoarse. Then he stopped again, resuming stroking her, building up the pleasure and yet withholding the final point.

"Please, Kahu…oh God, please… Please. Please…"

Begging. Dear God, she was begging. He brushed his fingers lightly over her pussy, watching her shiver. "You want more, sweetheart? Is that what you want?"

"Yes…please… More. Again." She pushed against his hand again, insistent.

"More pain?"

"God, yes. Anything. Anything you want to give me." Her voice was broken and rusty sounding, desperate. And he was breathing faster, harder. The wild feeling was back, bringing with it a sense of power. That sharp, clear focus.

He traced the red welts on her pale skin, marks that he'd left there. His marks on her.

How many times had he been marked by other people? How many times had other people taken pieces of him? Too many times to count. Yet no one had ever done vice versa. No one had ever given him a piece of themselves like Lily had.

But he wasn't content with just one piece. He wanted all of them. Every single one.

His hands closed on the tender flesh of one buttock and he squeezed, testing her. Did she know what she'd done? Did she know who'd she'd given herself to?

She cried out in response, arching.

It must have hurt and yet she didn't say her word. Still trusting him.

He smacked her with the flat of his hand, a sharp sound of flesh hitting flesh, and she flinched. "Are you sure, Lily?" he demanded, keeping his hand on her hot skin. "Are you sure you know what you're doing giving yourself to me like this?"

"Yes, God, yes." Her voice was thick, the last word catching on a sob.

"I'm a fucking prostitute. I'm a dirty rent boy. Are you sure that's what you want?"

"I don't care." The words were a whisper.

He smacked her again, a savagery filling him that was at the same time tempered by the brutal control he had on himself. He wanted to push her, make her understand who he was and yet give herself to him anyway, the broken person he was.

He didn't fucking deserve it but he didn't care. He'd take it anyway.

"I didn't hear you, ballerina. Say it." His palm descended again.

She gasped. "I said, I don't care."

"Louder." Another smack.

"I don't care!" The cry ended on another sob as he pressed his hand hard against her flesh.

"Why?" He squeezed her again, relentless. "You don't know how many cocks I've sucked. How many people I've fucked. How many people have fucked me. I'm used. I'm broken." He pushed his hand between her thighs, sliding two fingers inside her, her wetness coating him, stretching her deliberately. She wailed, a high, needy sound. "You can't save me, sweetheart, no one can save me. Why would you trust a man like me?"

He could hear her breath sobbing in her throat, her body moving helplessly against his hand, and he knew he should stop. Knew he'd pushed her too hard, too far. That she didn't deserve this kind of treatment. But there was a savage possessiveness tearing him up inside, a need he couldn't restrain. The need to own her, make her his completely in a way no one else had ever been.

You don't just want her surrender. You want her soul.

His heart squeezed hard inside his chest. No, he didn't want that. What would he do with her soul? This was a night, wasn't it? Nothing more.

"Because you're a good man," Lily said in a voice so croaky it sounded as if it had been scoured by steel wool. "Because you showed me what passion is. What pleasure is. Because you held me. Because you helped me feel not so fucking lonely." She took in a heaving breath. "I don't care who you were or what you've done or how many people you've fucked. You're not dirty. You're not broken. You're my music and music is pure. So that's what you are. You're pure, Kahu."

Barbed wire circled his soul and pulled tight. And he stood there, for a long moment unable to breathe. How could she say that? How could she see that in him? He wasn't pure. He'd never been fucking pure.

She shifted, starting to turn and reflexively he put his hand down in the small of her back, holding her down.

"No," he said hoarsely. "Stay there."

She stilled instantly but he could see the trembles shaking her. "Kahu…please. I need you. I want you so much. Please…."

He spread his hand out on her pale skin, the red marks of the flogger and his own blows showing up between his fingers. Fuck. If she thought he was pure, she really was holding nothing back.

Unlike you with Anita.

The barbed wire pulled even tighter. Broken, dirty and yet she wanted him.

Instinctive fear warred with the deep, crushing need, an animal tearing itself apart inside him. He felt like he could barely breathe.

"Keep still," he ground out then, pulling his hand away from her, he turned and went over to the coffee able, opening a drawer in the side of it and finding the small box where he kept a stash of condoms. He paused a couple of moments, fighting for a breath as he took one out of the box.

This needed to end. Now.

Dealing with the packet and trying to ignore his shaking hands, he sheathed himself then went back to where Lily was bent over. She shifted as he gripped her hips and positioned himself behind her, her back arching in anticipation, bright curls falling everywhere.

You can't keep her. You can never keep her.

No. He couldn't. She was far too young for him and he was far too broken for her, no matter what she thought about it. But he could mark her, make her remember. Imprint himself on her so she would never forget him or what she'd given him.

He would hurt her, but perhaps then she'd learn.

Sometimes distance was better. Sometimes distance was all you had.

Kahu pushed inside her, hard, deep.

She gave a hoarse little scream, her body stiffening, her pussy convulsing around his cock, clamping down hard as she came.

He closed his eyes, almost holding his breath because she was insanely hot and tight, and the temptation to let go of the leash was intense. But he held on, beginning to thrust, controlling the pace, feeling her pulse around him.

"Oh my God, oh my God…Kahu…" Shards of words falling around him, sharp and mirrored, reflecting back what he was doing to her, her pain and her pleasure. "So good, oh God… Oh Jesus…I can't…I don't think I can do this…"

He kept his eyes closed, kept pushing hard, faster, deeper. Hearing her pant, the words stopping, replaced by ragged sobs.

She's broken you. She's broken you.

But how could she do that? He was already broken. He'd been broken years ago.

He kept going, feeling her body gather for another climax and this time she didn't scream or sob, she only whimpered like a child.

By that time he couldn't hold on anymore, the vicious grip of his own climax beginning to tighten around him. As it did so, he pulled her upright, arm around her waist, the other across her chest, holding her steady as he drove himself into her body.

And when it pulled him apart, he buried his face in the bright softness of her hair, allowing himself one instant where it was all okay. Where she was his and he kept her safe forever.

Then he sunk his teeth into her shoulder, as the pleasure exploded through him.

Another mark before he let her go.

Chapter Thirteen

Lily was shaking and shaking and shaking. It felt like she'd never stop. Only the strength of Kahu's arms around her kept her upright. Jesus, if he let her go, she'd fall.

Her shoulder stung where he'd bitten her and her butt stung from the leather of the flogger and the blows from his hand. Her sex ached and she felt raw from the pleasure he'd given her. From the pain he'd wound inextricably with it.

Tears ran down her cheeks. Jesus, why was she crying? Yeah, she hurt, but he was right, there was good pain and it was all good pain. Wonderful pain.

He was hot against her back, so fucking hot. His arms so fucking strong. His mouth brushed over her shoulder then the nape of her neck, his breath warm. "Thank you." His voice roughened velvet. "Thank you for your gift, ballerina."

There was a subtle shift in his body and she whimpered, the sensation almost too much for her.

He hushed her, a hand stroking down her spine, soothing and light. Then there was another shift and his arms were around her, lifting her up like she weighed nothing. She didn't protest, turning her head against his chest, inhaling the musky, masculine scent of him. The second time he'd picked her up and carried her. God, she could get used to it so easily.

She didn't look to see where he was taking her, closing her eyes instead. Resting against him.

Another shift and she lifted her lids. They were in the bathroom and he was undressing her then lowering her into the bath. The water was still warm but as he got in with her, he turned the hot tap on again, a hot current against her skin.

She shivered, her whole body shaking at the sensation.

"Relax," he murmured, his arms coming around her, urging her to lie back against him.

So she did, her eyes drifting shut again, her muscles lax as he began to wash her, long, slow strokes down her arms and torso. Gentle movements down her legs and between her thighs. Caresses that didn't demand anything of her.

The combination of the water and Kahu's touch made her feel weightless, like she was floating.

It was so good to be touched like this. So good to feel cared for. She never wanted it to end.

And yeah, so she was crying, but that didn't matter. It was like all the shit she'd been dealing with for years was slowly being sloughed off as Kahu washed her, being cleaned away by his touch. All the loneliness and pain and fear that had hardened the outside of her, a shell that had kept the world at bay. Leaving her wiped clean. A brand new Lily.

"You're amazing," she murmured drowsily. "You're the most incredible man I've ever met."

"And exactly how many men have you met?" His voice was amused, his hands moving on her body, soothing her.

"Not many. But you're still amazing." She let her head fall back against his shoulder, arching as his hand settled on her stomach. Hell, she could *not* want more, could she? Surely after that, she wouldn't be able to take it.

"No," he murmured as if he'd read her mind. "I think you need to rest now."

She sighed. "Later?"

He didn't reply, his hands pushed into her hair, massaging her scalp and she gave a moan of pleasure. "Please say yes."

Only silence behind her, his hands maintaining a steady pressure.

A strange pain caught behind her breastbone. "Kahu?"

"Lie back, sweetheart."

"No." She sat up, water swirling around her, his hands falling away, and turned to him.

And the pain in her chest turned into a knife because the look on his face was guarded, his dark eyes opaque. Protecting himself again.

She'd given him everything. Her body, her trust.

And your stupid heart. Or are you going to ignore that too?

Lily took a silent, anguished breath. Yeah, she had given him that as well. She knew that now. And what was she getting in return? Walls. Shut doors.

What did you expect? That he was different? That you could put him back together when you can barely heal yourself?

"This is it, isn't it?" She hadn't meant the words to sound accusing, but they did.

His gaze didn't flicker and he didn't pretend to misunderstand. "I'm sorry, Lily."

It shouldn't hurt, but of course it did. And this time it wasn't good pain. It was bad. "What are you sorry about? We only said one night after all."

"We did. But I'm sorry because I hurt you."

Her throat felt thick, like she was coming down with a really fucking miserable cold. "It's okay, you didn't."

A breath escaped him. "You're crying, love."

"Don't call me that. I'm not your love." Her heart was beating faster now, anger coming to her rescue and thank God, because that was easier to deal with than this sharp, tearing pain.

Unable to bear the regret in his eyes, she turned away, putting her hands on the sides of the bath. "I want to get out now."

"Lily." His hands gripped her hips, holding her against him. "You don't have to go."

"Yeah, I do. Let go of me."

"Ballerina…"

"Let me go!" The words burst out, riddled with anguish. And instantly she felt his hands fall away from her.

Tears caught in her throat. With a surge, she pushed herself out of the bath, water overflowing onto the floor. She didn't turn to look at him, reaching to grab a towel, wrapping it around her.

"I'm sorry, Lily." His voice was hideous in its gentleness. "I never meant to hurt you."

She wanted to keep up the pretense, lift her chin and carry on. Ignore the hurt like she did when she was dancing, because the fucking show had to go on, didn't it?

But then again, why should she? Why should she pretend nothing was wrong? Pretending it didn't matter didn't make it hurt any less. She'd done it enough times with her father to know that.

She turned around to see that he'd gotten out too and was standing on the other side of the bath, wrapping a towel around his lean hips, that horrible, regretful look on his face. Like a parent denying a child a special treat.

"Well, you did," she said. "You did hurt me."

"I'm sorry."

"Stop saying that. It doesn't help."

He let out a breath. "I don't know what you expected. We agreed on one night. I didn't want anything more."

"I thought I didn't either." She swallowed against the pain in her throat. "Turns out I do."

Something crossed his face, an expression she couldn't read, like anger and desire and frustration all at the same time. "I can't give it to you, Lily. Whatever it is that you want, I can't give it."

She fought the knife twisting in her chest, the shivers that kept wracking her. It was true she was changing the rules on him, wanting more than they'd agreed on. But why not? Why shouldn't she want more? "Why can't you, Kahu? God, I'm not asking you to marry me or anything stupid like that. I just thought... This feels important, doesn't it? I mean, what's going on between us. It's different. Major."

The strange look on his face vanished. Wiped away as if it had never been. And then there was nothing but that jaded, cynical look, the one she thought she wouldn't have to see again. "Different? Oh sweetheart, that's the sex talking, I'm afraid." His beautiful voice was faintly mocking. "The truth is, it's nothing I haven't done many times before. Your reaction is quite usual and it'll fade in time."

She stared at him, shaky like a building suddenly without a foundation. "No. It's not like that. That wasn't... It was more than that."

"I know it felt that way. It's all new to you after all."

A tremble shook her, a wave of cold passing over her skin. "Don't," she said thickly. "Don't do that. I know what I felt. I know what you felt too. It was more. It was *important.*"

The expression on his face hardened, his eyes cold. She could almost see the distance he was opening up between them, a gulf as vast as oceans. "No, darling, it wasn't. You're just another in a long line of pretty girls I've fucked. It was good, you're right about that. But if you think you're the only woman I've bent over that couch and flogged, then you're mistaken."

It felt like he'd slapped her. She blinked, more hot tears filling her eyes. "I gave you everything. I gave you myself."

"I know you did. And believe me, I'm grateful. But call it a temporary loan that I'm now returning to you."

"You bastard." The tears slipped over her cheeks and this time she felt every one.

For a second the jaded expression disappeared, a moment of genuine sadness flickered over his face. "I never pretended I was anything different, ballerina. You only saw what you wanted to see."

A fucking ex-prostitute. A dirty rent boy.

That's how he thought of himself, wasn't it? That's what he saw. But she didn't see that. She'd never seen that.

Her anger began to fade, leaving behind it only the pain. What was the point in getting angry with him? He was only protecting himself the way he always did.

"I know what I saw, Kahu" she whispered. "But I'm not the one who's being blind."

She saw the barb land home, the flare in his dark eyes. Then he looked away.

He didn't trust her, she could see that. Perhaps he didn't trust anyone, and maybe, with a background like his, he never would. His defenses were meters thick, there was no way she'd get through them and she was a fool to think otherwise.

Anyway, the kinds of hurts he must have suffered took years to recover from. Did she really think one night of sex would heal everything?

Lily didn't know where she found the strength, but somehow she did, dropping the towel on the floor and picking up her crumpled dress. Then she walked naked to the door, her heart in broken pieces in her chest. But then life was pain, wasn't it? That was the beauty of the dance.

She paused in the doorway and looked at him. So tall, powerful. Beautiful. Yet so dreadfully alone. There was one piece of herself she hadn't given him yet and despite everything he thought about himself, he deserved to have it.

"You want to know who I saw?" she said quietly. "I saw the man I fell in love with. And if you can't see that man too, then that's a loss for both of us."

She didn't wait for him to reply, walking through the door into the bedroom where there was still wine and food from the snack he'd brought them.

The sight hurt but she didn't hesitate, going on through to the lounge where the rest of her scattered clothes were.

She dressed, her hands shaking, hoping he would follow, knowing he wouldn't.

And he didn't.

There was no sound as she opened the door of his apartment.

No sound at all when she closed it.

"Jesus," Eleanor said, frowning at him. "You're a wreck. What happened?"

Kahu reached for the wine in front of him. Christ, he hated wine. Why was he drinking this shit? He swallowed the rest in his glass but it did nothing for the burning sensation in his chest. The one that hadn't gone away since Lily had walked out of his bedroom two weeks earlier.

"Nothing," he said, trying for lazy and getting only curt. "I'm a little under the weather."

"Bullshit you are." She narrowed her gaze. "What's going on, Kahu? You look like your best friend just died. And since I'm still alive and so are Connor and Victoria, it's not that."

Around them the club continued its usual noisy, lunchtime business. It had never irritated him more, the happy, laughing people going about their lives. As if nothing touched them.

Really, he should be one of them. Except for some reason, he couldn't find his usual humor, his usual mockery. The comfortable, casual mask of easy cynicism had vanished and he didn't know where it had gone.

Of course you fucking know. Lily took it with her when she left.

Shit no. He wasn't going to think of Lily. Of the pain in her eyes as he'd systematically stripped their night together of any significance and turned it into another round of mediocre, emotionless screwing. As he changed her into merely another woman he'd fucked. Putting so much distance between them there could be no coming back from it.

He'd had to. She wasn't his and she could never be and that was the end to the matter.

Kahu pushed the glass away and reached under the bar for the bottle again. Then felt Eleanor's cool hand on his. He looked up and met her eyes, seeing the concern in them. "What?" he demanded, gracelessly.

"Who is it?" A pause. "Or rather, who is she?"

He jerked his hand away. "What are you talking about?"

But his friend's gaze was inescapable. "I know that look, Kahu. Believe me, I know. I used to see it in my mirror a lot when I got together with Luc. You're in love, aren't you?"

"Love? Seriously? Me? Fuck off."

Eleanor let out a breath. "Who is it? Come on, don't be a prick. I came to you for Luc advice, which turned out okay in the end, luckily for you."

"I'm not in love. Christ, where the hell would you get that idea from? You know me. I don't fall in love. I'm not built for it." The words tasted hard and gritty in his mouth, like stones. Like lies.

His friend only looked at him then sighed. "Have it your way."

But of course she was right.

He was in love. And he had been since the day Lily took off her clothes and danced naked. Maybe even since the day she'd got out the chessboard because she'd watched him play and thought he might like it.

A silence fell, heavy with the weight of everything he wanted and didn't have the courage to reach for.

"I can't have her," he said at last, helplessly. "She's too young. Too bright. Too brave and too fucking beautiful. She's Rob's daughter and she's twenty. I'm thirty-eight. I'm a fucking ex-prostitute. I've got nothing to offer her but this stupid club. What would she want with that? With me?"

Eleanor was silent a long time. "Does she love you?"

You're my music, Kahu.

"Yes." The word was hoarse and broken. "Silly girl that she is."

"And do you love her?"

If you can't see that man, then that's a loss for both of us.

"Yes." Again hoarse. Again broken.

"Then that's what you have to offer her."

He looked up at last and there was understanding in her eyes. And sympathy. "She's too good for me, Ell. What if it's not enough?"

She smiled. "It's always enough, Kahu."

Surely she was wrong. It hadn't been enough for Anita. Or at least, his love hadn't been enough.

This isn't the same.

No, it wasn't. Because this time, he knew Lily loved him. She'd said it. Out loud. To his face. Her green-gray eyes full of pain and truth as sharp as knives

And this time it was him who was pulling away. Him who kept himself separate and holding back. This time he was Anita.

You coward.

"She's too young," he said again. "She's Rob's fucking daughter."

"So? Who cares about that? Luc's way too young for me but he doesn't give a shit. And neither do I." Eleanor gave him a look he didn't much like. "You want to know what I think?"

"Not particularly."

"Those are excuses, Kahu. Weren't you the one who told me people who are scared use excuses to hide behind?"

"No. It must have been some other stupid, fucking idiot."

"There's only one stupid, fucking idiot who told me that and I'm looking at him right now."

But it wasn't until he'd gotten back to his apartment that night, and was struck yet again, as he had been for the past two weeks, by the emptiness of it, by the sheer lack of a small, slender yet impossibly strong ballet dancer, that he understood Eleanor was right.

He was a stupid fucking idiot.

He didn't know how and he didn't know why, but he'd fallen in love with Lily and she wasn't here. She wasn't goddamned here and he couldn't stand it. All he could see was her pale, delicate face, determined as always. Giving him the last piece of herself.

I see the man I've fallen in love with.

Laying herself open to him. Laying herself bare. Giving him her soul.

Why couldn't he accept it? Why couldn't he give her his in return? Why did the thought fill him with absolute terror?

It was Anita, of course. He'd done what Lily had and had it thrown back in his face.

But did you really do what Lily did?

In the process of getting himself a glass of scotch, he stopped, staring at the empty glass in his hand.

Had he? Had he ever laid himself open to Anita like that? Had he given her everything of himself the way Lily had done?

Then again, he knew the answer to that question, didn't he? He knew the answer deep down. No, he hadn't. He'd let her do the culture, the food, the education, all the things she'd wanted. But he'd never once told her no. Never told her that he didn't like it. Never told her what he *did* want.

Because first he'd been too scared. And then he'd been too angry.

Scared from years on the streets where he'd divorced his mind from his body, protecting himself the only way he could by never revealing anything, keeping everything he was close and safe, his emotions completely detached.

Angry because he'd needed her to get rid of her armor first. And she hadn't.

And then she'd let him go.

Like Lily had let him go.

The glass fell from his hand and smashed on the floor.

He could have gone after Anita. He could have refused to leave when she'd told him too. If only he'd risked himself for her. If only he'd been braver.

Now he had the same choice. To let Lily go because he wasn't brave enough to hold on to what he wanted. Or learn from her strength and her determination. To not surrender.

To fight.

You're my music, Kahu.

His heart swelled up inside his chest, full and painful with need, with desire. Oh, holy fucking God, he wanted to be her music. Wanted to be the man she thought she saw. His would be a dirty kind of music maybe, out of tune and off-key. Hard to listen to, harder to dance to. But he would be there, surrounding her, supporting her, a soundtrack she could maybe live her life to.

All he had to do was give her everything he was. Not just his body, not just his passion. He had to give her his heart too. Because if he didn't…

You'll always be broken.

Kahu turned from the broken glass at his feet, ignoring it completely, and pulled his phone from his pocket, punched in a number.

"Hey Rob," Kahu said. "Sorry to call you so late, but I need to talk to you about Lily."

She wasn't nervous, though perhaps she should have been. There were a number of people sitting at the table in the large, airy room, looking at her with polite but distant smiles on their faces.

They'd specified a black leotard so that's what she wore. To make herself stand out, she'd put on a black headband with a dark green *koru* pattern on it—a uniquely Maori fern design. For her New Zealand roots of course, nothing to do with Kahu.

Not that she'd thought about him once during the last two weeks of frantic lessons and practice before she flew to Sydney for the private audition that had been offered to her the week before. Of course she hadn't. She'd been far, far too fucking busy.

The director indicated for her to start so she prepared herself as the music flooded the room.

Why wasn't she nervous? She always had been before, especially with something as important as this. Because if she failed again and didn't get in….

You'd what?

Lily rose up on her toes and lifted her arms, and began to dance.

And abruptly she was back in Kahu's study, dancing for him. Dancing naked, with his gaze on her, so hungry and intent. Freeing something within herself, the passion that had always been there that cancer had taken from her.

She spun, ran and leapt, the music around her, over her, propelling her into the air then catching her as she came down again. Like Kahu had. With his hands on her body and his dark, husky voice.

She lifted her leg, turned toward the directors with her arms out. But she didn't see them. She only saw a dark-eyed man who'd watched her dance. Who'd made her fall in love with him.

Oh, she knew why she wasn't nervous. Because this didn't matter. The audition, the career, the lost years she'd spent being sick, none of it mattered. And even if she failed here, if she never danced again, she wouldn't have lost anything.

It was the passion that mattered. The passion for dance, for life, for love. The passion for living and it had been here all along. It was inside her, burning bright and strong.

She held the passion within herself and nothing, not failure, not losing, not even fucking cancer could ever take that away.

Lily threw her arms out and lost herself to that passion, to the music flowing through her, and to the memory of Kahu's hands on her body, lifting her up into the sky, launching her so she could fly.

And when the music died and she opened her eyes and came back to herself, she found she was facing the directors, her heart pumping, adrenaline effervescent in her blood. They stared back and she thought she saw shock on their faces.

She smiled because this didn't matter. They didn't matter.

There was only one thing that did.

That night, in her shitty Sydney hotel room, she took out her phone and scrolled through her contact list to find Kahu's number. She debated texting him then decided not to. A personal visit was better. She would dance for him again, convince him somehow that what they had was worth fighting for. Because he was worth fighting for. The dark passion that lived in him wasn't dirty or broken. It was as pure as hers. He just needed to see it.

It was as she was getting out of the shower that a knock came on her door. Puzzled, she squinted through peephole and saw one of the hotel employees outside. Weird. She wasn't expecting anyone.

As she pulled open the door, the guy smiled at her and handed her a box.

"For you, miss. I was asked to bring it to you."

This was not getting any less weird. She thanked him, took the box and closed the door. Then walked into the middle of the room and lifted the lid.

And her heart nearly stopped beating.

In the middle on a pillow of black velvet was a piece of greenstone. A familiar piece of greenstone.

Kahu's.

She swallowed, lifting it from the box and a piece of paper fell out as she did so.

Her hand shaking, Lily bent and picked up the paper. There was writing on it.

I'm in the bar and I have something to say. If you want to talk to me, come down and wear the necklace. If all you want is to say goodbye, come down but don't wear the necklace. If you never want to see me again, don't come down and throw the necklace away.

Your choice, ballerina. I'll live with whatever you decide.

He was here. He was here in Sydney. Oh fuck. Oh Jesus.

Lily's hands gripped the flax cord and they were still shaking as they drew the necklace over her head.

Kahu had never been so nervous in all his life. He sat at the bar in the extremely shitty Sydney hotel where Lily was staying, and he simply could not keep still. His fingers drummed on the wood and he hadn't even taken one sip of the scotch he'd ordered.

He didn't know what he would do if she didn't come. Well, he'd go back to Auckland heart-fucking-broken obviously, but after that? He had no idea.

It felt like his whole life had narrowed to this one point. This one woman. This choice he'd made.

The absence of the familiar weight of his necklace was like the absence of a limb. Remembered and still sensed but gone. A phantom.

If she didn't come down, he'd live with that absence forever. Except it wouldn't be the necklace he would be without, but the woman. A woman who'd stormed into his life, turned it upside down, turned him inside out, and whom he'd sent away because she scared the shit out of him.

A woman he wanted desperately.

He'd never be good enough for her, not in a hundred million fucking years. But he hoped what Eleanor had said would be true. That his love would be enough.

A movement by the bar door. Kahu looked, his heart contracting painfully in his chest. But it wasn't her. It was someone else.

He looked down into his scotch feeling like someone had stabbed him.

A hand came to rest lightly on his shoulder.

He turned sharply and looked into the eyes of the woman standing next to him. A color caught between green and gray, smoky and dark and yet somehow luminous. Her face was pale and anxious, her hair hanging in damp strawberry blonde curls around her shoulders. She wore jeans and a black top, and hanging between her small breasts was a familiar piece of greenstone.

Kahu stared at her and every single word he'd been going to say vanished from his head.

She was here and she was wearing his necklace.

"Lily," he forced out.

For a moment she stared at him so fiercely it was like she was committing every part of him to memory. Then she held out her hand.

Wordlessly, he took it and wordlessly, he followed her where she led him, up in the elevators, the space between them violent with everything he was desperate to say, desperate to do, then finally along the hallway to her door.

She opened it and he went in, and when she closed it he couldn't wait any more.

One step took him to her side, another and she was pressed against the closed door, his body fitting itself against her small, slender body. His hands cupping her face, the warmth of her skin like sun on the frozen ground of his body, waking him up, calling him back to life.

She didn't move and she didn't protest, and he knew he'd overstepped the line but he just couldn't bring himself to move away. Not yet.

"I'm sorry," he said in a voice he didn't recognize as his. "I'm sorry I said those things to you, ballerina. I didn't mean them, not any of them. This does matter and this is important and you're the only woman in the world I want."

He should let her go. But he didn't. He covered her mouth, kissed her until the taste of her filled his head and eased the terrible ache that had taken up residence inside him. Then he lifted his head.

Lily's face was flushed, her pouty mouth full and red. And she smiled. She fucking smiled. "Hello, Kahu, nice to see you too."

"I'm not sorry."

"For kissing me? God, I hope not." Her hands came to rest on his chest, a gentle pressure. "What are you doing here?"

"I wanted to apologize for what I said to you when you left. And I wanted to tell you that you were right, I've been blind. I've been blind for fucking years. I've been closing myself off, isolating myself. Protecting myself. Because I've been too fucking scared to let anyone in." He stared down into her eyes, saw her bright soul staring back. "Those years on the streets broke me and I thought… Christ, Lily, I thought the only way to stop myself from being broken anymore, the only way to keep myself safe, was to not let anyone touch me. Not let anyone take any more pieces of my soul. But then you came and you got under my skin, got under my defenses." He stroked the soft skin of her jaw. "You touched me, ballerina. With your strength and your passion, and your sheer bloody-mindedness. I have no protection against you, none at all." He took a breath and then made himself stand away to give her space.

It was the hardest thing he'd ever had to do in his life.

"You told me I was pure. That I was your music. Well, I'm a hideous kind of music, sweetheart. But I want to play for you. I want to be there to lead you through the dance. To watch you move and grow and change. See you be the superstar you are." His voice had grown hoarse but he went on anyway. "I love you, ballerina. You have my heart and you have my soul. You have all the dirty pieces of me there are. Take them, Lily. I don't want them anymore. They're yours."

A tear slipped down her cheek, a tiny jewel. "No," she said fiercely. "You're not dirty. None of those pieces of you are. You had to do some really crappy things, but you did them to protect your family and you did them to survive. You fought, Kahu. And you came through. That doesn't mean you're broken. That means you're strong." She came forward and put a hand on his chest, her touch a stroke deep inside him. "Do you know what happened today? I had my audition. And as I was dancing, I realized something. That it didn't matter. Whether I got a place in the company or whether I failed. Whether I dance again or whether I don't.

It doesn't matter. What matters is passion, is heart. And it's here, it's inside me." Another tear joined the first. "You showed me that, Kahu. You taught me what it was. That's where my strength comes from and that's where yours lives too."

His throat closed up and it was hard to speak. Hard to articulate the great, crushing emotion that gripped him. "Fuck," he forced out. "You're only twenty. How the hell did you get to be so wise?"

Lily's hand slid up his chest, curled around his neck. "I had a good teacher. Plus living with death for three years changes your perspective a little."

"Who was your teacher?"

"You, you idiot." Then she pulled his mouth down on hers and he discovered she was right. Nothing else mattered but this.

Sometime in the night, when they were finally sated and panting, Lily lay back in Kahu's arms and put her hand on the necklace still lying between her breasts. "You're never getting this back, okay?"

"I told you, greenstone can only be given. And it's yours now."

"Excellent." She snuggled against him, running a hand down his hard body.

He groaned. "Jesus, woman. I'm an old man. Give me a moment."

She laughed. "Please don't tell me I'm going to have to break out the Viagra. You're not that old."

At that moment her cell phone rang. She debated not answering it but then Kahu nudged her. "You should get that. I think I know who it might be."

She turned in his arms, looking up at him. "Who?"

"Your dad."

"Oh?"

"I told him about us."

Oh.

"It was probably premature," Kahu went on, "seeing as how I called him before I left for Sydney or spoke to you, but I wanted him to know."

"Good," Lily said firmly. "I'm glad you did."

She rolled out of bed and reached for the phone, and punched the answer button. She wasn't nervous about this, of course she wasn't. "Hey Dad."

A small silence. "Lily," her father said. "How did the audition go?"

So he'd remembered that, had he? "I don't know. They're going to let me know in the next week or so."

Another silence. "I'm...proud of you, you know that?"

Her throat felt tight. "Um...no, actually, I didn't know. It's not like you tell me."

Her father sighed. "I'm sorry, Lily. I've been a pretty crap father for a long time, haven't I?"

Lily swallowed. "Yeah, Dad. You have."

"Look, I know I can't make up for that. But...Kahu talked to me about... Well, about the fact that you and he are...you know."

"Having an affair?"

"Yes, that."

Her hand clenched tight on the phone. "We're not having an affair, Dad. We're in love."

"I have to tell you that you should keep away from him. He's a good man but his past—"

"I know all about his past. And it doesn't matter."

Her father was silent. Then he said, "Stay away anyway, Lily. Love is…painful."

There was a warm hand on her back, a warm mouth on her shoulder. Kahu's music, keeping her strong. "Love is a good kind of pain, Dad. Didn't you know that? And if we didn't have pain, how would we understand happiness?"

"Oh, ballerina." Kahu's voice, low and quiet behind her. "I don't know if your father can handle that right now."

And there was more silence on the end of the phone. "He's with you now, isn't he?"

"Yes," Lily said. "And I'm never leaving him, Dad. He's mine. Now if you'll excuse me, we have some urgent stuff to attend to." She hung up the call and threw the phone onto the floor. And turned into Kahu's arms.

And there was music, and pain and pleasure.

And above all, there was love.

About the Author

Jackie has been writing fiction since she was eleven years old. Mild mannered fantasy/SF/pseudo-literary writer by day, obsessive romance writer by night, she used to balance her writing with the more serious job of librarianship until a chance meeting with another romance writer prompted her to throw off the shackles of her day job and devote herself to the true love of her heart—writing romance. She particularly likes to write dark, emotional stories with alpha heroes who've just got the world to their liking only to have it blown wide apart by their kick-ass heroines.

She lives in Auckland, New Zealand with her husband, the inimitable Dr. Jax, two kids, two cats and some guppies (possibly dead guppies by the time you read this). When she's not torturing alpha males and their stroppy heroines, she can be found drinking chocolate martinis, reading anything she can lay her hands on, posting random crap on her blog, or being forced to go mountain biking with her husband.

You can find Jackie at www.jackieashenden.com or follow her on Twitter @JackieAshenden.

Finding his way out of the darkness could be the biggest fight of his life.

Living in Shadow
© 2014 Jackie Ashenden

Living In…, Book 1

Law professor Eleanor May is fine with taking over a class for a colleague on sabbatical. She's not so fine with the hot student who's always seated front and center. Once upon a time *she* was that student… and the scars remain eight years after it ended.

Yet this guy seems different from the others. Despite the alarm bells in her head warning her about history repeating itself, she is drawn toward the forbidden once again—even though this time it could consume her.

Lucien North's past is darker than the ink on his skin, a reminder of a time when survival was a fight to the death. Seducing his beautiful professor wasn't supposed to be part of his plan to put it behind him, but there's something about Eleanor that's gotten hold of him and won't let go.

Together they light up the night, but will their powerful desire lead them to love—or drag them both to the brink of disaster?

Warning: This book contains a younger man so hot he might scorch your fingertips, and forbidden lust so tempting, there's no point in trying to resist. Check your inhibitions at the door—it's WTFery 101 and class is in session.

Available now in ebook and print from Samhain Publishing.

Wine her, dine her…then untie her.

Sweet Obsession
© *2014 Kelly Jamieson*

Windy City Kink, Book 1

Sasha Bendel is a bundle of nerves as she knocks on the door of a Gold Coast penthouse. Her landscape design business took a hard hit when one of her biggest clients defaulted on his payment, and she desperately needs this rooftop garden design project to get back in the black.

But when her potential client answers the door, she's stunned. It's her old high school boyfriend, the one her wealthy parents ran out of her life when they were discovered engaging in some youthful exploration of bondage and discipline.

Twelve years ago, Jack Grenville let Sasha's powerful father intimidate him into giving up the love of his life. With the help of a sensei, he's overcome his obstacles and accepted his sexual dominance. Now he's back in Chicago to claim what's his—Sasha.

One look at Jack brings back all the forbidden desires Sasha's put on lock-down since that shameful night. No way can she turn down this money-is-no-object job…but can she resist Jack's no-knots-barred determination to recapture her heart?

Warning: This book contains a woman with a sweet tooth, a man with a sweet obsession, a cupboard full of bondage rope, and some not-so-sweet kink.

Available now in ebook and print from Samhain Publishing.

SAMHAIN PUBLISHING

It's all about the story...

Romance

HORROR

Retro ROMANCE

www.samhainpublishing.com

CPSIA information can be obtained at www.ICGtesting.com
Printed in the USA
BVOW08s0641060815

411937BV00002B/68/P

9 781619 228252